THE FAMILY TREE

Sandra Lee Churchill

The Family Tree /Sandra Lee Churchill — 1st ed.

ISBN 978-0-6152-0464-2

For Mark, Stephanie, Brittany, and Timothy with love and gratitude — for filling my own tree with light, laughter, and joy.

SLC

CONTENTS

**Chapter One
The Announcement**

I should have known it was coming. Things were going too well. The day was too perfect. The mall was fun, the movie was pretty good, school was getting off to a great start, my teacher was cool, and my best friend Marcy was in all of my classes. Marcy says it's the Virgo in me. You know, the worrier, the planner, the pessimist who keeps looking for the down side in every situation... She's probably right. Marcy's a totally classic Gemini—fun, creative, disorganized, and happy—I mean, all the time. It would be annoying if she weren't my best friend. Well, more annoying. At least she brings me along for the ride.

"Thanks Mrs. Montgomery," I said, slamming the car door and waving to Marcy. My heart still pounded a little as I crossed into the shadows on the front walk. At twelve and a half, I knew it was silly, but I always felt compelled to run up my driveway when it was dark. Even the yellow porch light didn't do much to scare away my fears about some nut jumping out at me from behind the tall rhododendron shrubs in front of our house. Marcy and her Mom waited on the street until I slipped my key in the lock.

I looked back to see Marcy and her mom blink their headlights at me and made my way into the house. Surprised to see Mom and Josh sitting on the living room couch, I plopped down on the piano bench. I was so spooked running up the driveway that I didn't notice his truck parked outside. They looked up and smiled when I entered the room. The light was dimmed and the television was turned off. Mom looked pretty in a flowery dress and red cardigan sweater. Josh was dressed up too, in a white shirt and black pants.

"Hi," I said.

2

"Hello, Cass" they said in almost perfect unison.

Something must be up. But they were smiling at me so I knew I wasn't in trouble.

"What's up?" I asked casually.

"How was the movie?"

The movie. They wanted to know about the movie. "Fine," I answered. "Not as good as the first one though."

"Sequels hardly ever are," Josh chimed in.

"So what's the special occasion? You're both all dressed up. Did you guys go out tonight?"

"Well," Mom began slowly. "We had a candlelight dinner at home. Josh cooked for me."

The smile lingered on Mom's face. She looked like she had something to say.

"What's up?", I asked.

"We'll ..." Mom said, still smiling. "We have some news."

"News?" I wondered what kind of news. My heart skipped a beat—a job change? We were moving? A vacation?

Mom saved me from endless guessing.

"Honey, Josh and I are engaged."

"Engaged?" I said, forgetting to smile. "When?"

3

Mom came over and put her arm around me. "Tonight. Josh just asked me tonight."

"Wow", I said in disbelief. "Congratulations."

Engaged. It seemed so sudden but, I guessed it would happen sometime. Josh was good to Mom. He stood up and smiled at Mom and me.

I turned Mom's hand over and inspected her ring. It looked like a teardrop. "That's pretty," I said, staring at the diamond. The soft living room light made the ring sparkle all the more.

"How do you feel, honey?" Mom nudged me and whispered in my ear.

Josh took the hint and headed for the kitchen.

"Okay," I whispered. "I mean, surprised." I smiled so Mom wouldn't be disappointed, then hugged her.

Through the doorway, I called out another "Congratulations!" to Josh, who was making puttering sounds in the kitchen.

"Thanks, Cass." He stepped into the doorway, for a minute, a tall shadow framed in the kitchen light.

"Have you told Ben?" I asked suddenly. My eight year-old little brother had been forgotten until now.

"No, he was already in bed. I'll tell him in the morning," said Mom, reassuringly. "Let me talk to him first, okay?"

"Oh, I won't say anything. Can we talk some more later? I'm really tired so I think I'll just go to bed."

Mom touched my shoulder. "You're okay, Cassie?"

I nodded. "Fine, Mom. I'm just tired." I moved toward the kitchen, not wanting to be rude to Mom, but using a goodnight to Josh as an excuse to escape. I needed some time.

"Goodnight Josh," I called without seeing him. "And congratulations again."

"Thanks."

"You too, Mom," I said quietly, heading for the stairs.

"Good night honey," she said. "Sleep well."

Josh's voice echoed from the kitchen as I made my way upstairs and down the hall toward my room. "Don't let the bed bugs bite."

***

Morning came before long and it was Saturday. No school. No homework. From my bed the day looked sunny. Then I remembered the "news" Mom had told me last night. Things would be even more different, more changed. Getting used to Dad not being here was hard enough, but a new father? Josh was great as Mom's boyfriend, but I just couldn't picture him as a Dad. Never mind that my own father wasn't around much lately.

I thought about Josh as I slipped into my favorite pair of jeans and a funky lime green sweater that Marcy had convinced me would look great with my eyes. He had so much energy. You'd swear he was a kid in a grown-up's body. He threw the ball around with Ben and had tons of time to play in our yard after supper when he came over. Still—he wasn't our Dad. Then again, he wasn't like some of my friends' fathers either. Josh was fun and he had always made time for us — more time than Dad had made for Ben and me.

All this thinking made me hungry and nervous at the same time. I shoved my feet into sneakers with the laces still tied and headed for breakfast. Mom and Ben were already at the kitchen table—Ben with his bowl of cornflakes and three cereal boxes barricading him into a little hide-away and Mom talking over the boxes while she poured him some juice. They must have just come down because Mom didn't have her coffee cup out yet.

"Morning—" I said, pulling a box away from Ben to pour myself some cereal.

"No way! Gimme that back." He grabbed at the box.

"Hermit." I tossed it to him and made him catch it before the cereal spilled out.

"Have you told him yet?" I asked Mom as I pulled out a chair and slid into the seat against the wall.

She looked sleepy. "No, but I was just about to."

"Tell me what?" Ben grumbled behind his boxes.

"I have some news to tell you, about Josh and me. We were going to tell you last night but you were already asleep. Honey, Josh and I are getting married."

"Oh," was all he said. Then after a few seconds, sounding much more alert, "So he gets to live here then?"

"Yes. He'll move in with us after we get married."

"Cool!"

"Do you have anything you want to ask me, Ben? Anything you want to talk about?"

"No," he shrugged.

I stared at him from my chair, unable to say anything.

Mom leaned over to kiss Ben on top of his head. "So you're happy about Josh and me getting married?"

He spoke with his mouth full of cereal. "Sure. Josh is great."

Mom smiled. "He is, honey. That's why I love him so much."

I couldn't believe what I was hearing. Did he have a clue what this really meant? A new father? Eyeing my half-empty bowl, I snatched at one of his barricade boxes again, more to tick him off than because I really wanted seconds on cereal.

"Give it back!" he yelled.

"Don't be so selfish!" I snapped, making a dramatic show of pouring more cereal into my bowl, and deliberately leaving the box next to me.

"Cassie—gimme the box now!"

"Get it yourself," I mumbled, ignoring Mom's annoyed expression. If he was such a traitor to forget Dad just like that, I wasn't going to make life any easier for him.

Feeling myself getting angrier, I decided to ignore Ben and let him sulk behind the boxes. I could see his face through the little gap in his barricade—until he stood up and snatched the box back to finish his precious little hide-out that walled him off from the rest of the breakfast table.

"Mom?" I said, needing to be blunt. "Josh is nice and all, but I don't want a new father. Ben and I don't need one. We already have Dad." There, I said it—short and simple. Suddenly, I didn't much care if I hurt Mom's feelings. She certainly didn't think about mine before slipping that ring on her finger. She had asked me *afterwards*. What good was that? She had already decided. Her mind was made up. It was finished.

The calmness in her voice surprised me. "Oh, Cassie. Josh doesn't expect to be your Dad. Your father will always be your Dad. Josh knows that. He would never try to replace him. That's not the way he is."

"How do you know?"

"Because we've discussed this—a lot. Josh and I love each other and he loves you both very much. Trust me, honey. He cares about you and Ben and wants all four of us to become a family. That doesn't mean your father has been replaced. If it will make you feel better, you can talk to Josh about it and hear it straight from him."

I considered this. "I don't know," was all I could say. "Maybe."

"Cassie, it might feel a little uncomfortable for awhile, but these things take time. That doesn't mean you can't make room in your heart for Josh too. Do you like him?"

"Of course I like him. I just never thought about him being my father."

"Well, he's not. You have nothing to worry about." Her voice softened. "He's not out to replace anybody, sweetheart. He's just an addition to our family, so it's okay to like him as you already have. We just have to make room for him in our family. Everything will be all right. You'll see."

But I didn't see. Not completely. I saw only part of what she meant. What about all of the "father" things that happen in a home? Who yells at us when we do something wrong?

Who mows the lawn and fixes things and hangs his clothes next to Mom's in the big closet? It was weird enough having Dad out of the house, but still around once in awhile to help out now and then. He could still yell at us on the phone or during one of his visits if he needed to. So what about a new guy living here all the time? In my mind, those are still Dad's jobs and it'll be hard seeing Josh taking over.

Couldn't Mom see it wasn't going to be easy? Was I just being a pain or was I right to notice it would be difficult? I didn't want to hurt Mom but somebody had to tell her things would be strange. Ben certainly wasn't going to be the one. He just thought it was cool that his buddy Josh was coming to live with us. He didn't get it. Everything was changing and there was nothing we could do to stop it.

***

I called Marcy later that afternoon. We had decided last night to hit the mall today, and Mom would drive us over. I wanted to tell her the "news" first, in case Mom mentioned it in the car.

"Hello, Marcy?"

"Hi, Cass. What's up?"

"I have some news I wanted to tell you before we come to pick you up. Guess what?"

"What?"

"Mom and Josh got engaged last night."

"They did? Great! He's so nice. Are you happy?"

I hesitated. "Yeah, I'm happy. He is great, but it's gonna be strange having him live here like a new father."

"Well, you'll still see your Dad on some weekends, right?"

"I think so."

"Then you'll get to have both. Josh is fun and you can see him and do things a lot. But you and Ben will still get to see your Dad too."

What—had she been talking to my mom? As usual, my best friend was right. Marcy had a way of putting things into perspective. I never thought of Josh moving in as a bonus. He wasn't replacing Dad. Maybe he was just adding to our family. We'd get both.

"I never thought about it that way."

"Yeah. It'll be okay. You've always said you liked him. Hey — he could be some mean guy who hates kids, but he's awesome."

"I know. Guess it'll be all right."

Marcy skipped to the big day. "When's the wedding?"

"I don't know yet. Probably soon. I'll have to ask Mom."

I could kick myself for forgetting to ask something so basic.

"Do you get to be in the wedding?"

I hadn't thought about this either. She was great at sorting these things out. "I don't know."

"Well *ask*, silly. If you are, then we could help pick out the dresses and you get to wear fancy earrings and carry flowers and walk around in really high heels."

Leave it to Marcy to find a reason for shopping. She was right, though. It could be fun helping Mom plan the wedding. "Yeah. I'll talk to Mom. This might be fun!"

"Of course!"

We planned to pick her up in an hour and I hung up the phone. Maybe I could talk to Mom before we go so Marcy and I could check out the dresses at the mall. I knew it was Mom's choice, but it would be fun just to look.

***

Mom was nowhere to be found in the house so I checked the yard. She was out back digging in the garden. There was a pile of bulbs beside her that would be transplanted to the front yard so Josh could help us plant a vegetable garden next summer. They looked like daffodil bulbs but you never could be sure when they were just roots and there weren't any flowers on them. They just looked like little onions attached to some sprouts. Mystery flowers, I thought. Could be red, could be yellow. Nature's surprise—like the time Ben had peeled off the labels on a couple dozen cans just to see what would happen. He liked the shiny metal, but we ended up "adventure-eating" for a month, not knowing if the side dish was string beans, chicken noodle soup, or apple pie filling.

"Hi Mom. How's it going?"

She tugged hard at a stubborn weed, grunting as she plucked it out of the ground. "This is tougher than it looks," she sighed.

"It looks pretty hard. Do you need some help?"

She pushed up the edge of her polka-dotted gardening glove and peeked at her watch. "No, it'll be time to go pretty soon and you don't want to be all muddy for the mall. I'll be done in a few minutes. This is a good start for the garden."

"It'll be great," I said, scanning the rows of empty soil. "Do you think we could plant strawberries?"

"I don't see why not. How about we talk to Josh about the easiest things to grow? He's a gardening whiz and I don't want you kids disappointed if you spend all your time digging and watering and nothing comes up. Let's see what's a good crop to start out with."

"Okay."

I squatted down next to Mom. "When is the wedding going to be?"

"Not for a little bit. Since he's a teacher, Josh gets time off in the summer so it will probably be the end of June or early July, once the school year is out. That'll leave some time for a honeymoon."

"Where are you going?"

"I don't know yet. We haven't planned that far ahead."

"Oh. Will I get to be in the wedding?"

Mom looked surprised. "Would you want it to be a fancy wedding like that with bridesmaids and tuxedos?"

I shrugged. "I don't know. I just wondered."

"Well people don't usually have fancy ceremonies if it's a second wedding, but it can still be nice. We'll just plan something simple and ask our immediate family to come. Nothing too big, just the people close to us."

She looked over at me. Her eyes sparkled. "We can go shopping for a new dress for you to wear."

"Okay," I said. I felt better already. It would be special but it wouldn't be big or strange. The wedding would be small — a family party. I wondered if Marcy would be disappointed. I'd be dressed up but not a real bridesmaid.

"If you want, Cass, we can make some of the plans together. You can help me decide on the food and the music—"

"Sure, Mom."

"It's going to be fine. Come talk to me about anything, okay? I know this is awkward, but don't be afraid to tell me if you're upset or confused. This can be a tough transition for a family. But I'm always here for you."

I nodded, grateful she was trying to make this easier on me. "I love you, Mom," I said, turning and making my way back toward the house. It was almost time to pick up Marcy for our mall spree.

"I love you too, honey," Mom answered over my shoulder.

Her words echoed over and over in my head as I walked across the yard. "It's going to be fine, it's going to be fine, it's going to be fine..."

Chapter Two
The Assignment

"People?" Mrs. Frazier clapped her hands. "People, take your seats. Mr. Stevenson? Mr. MacPherson? Please take your seats. Your conversation will have to wait until later."

Marcy giggled and whispered something about Brad looking cute today. I looked over at Keith and Brad as they dragged themselves to their desks. Brad did look adorable today. He wore a purple, long-sleeved polo shirt and jeans. His braces sparkled when he smiled. Brad and Keith were always getting in trouble, but nothing really bad ever happened in Mrs. Frazier's class. She was pretty cool. Not like Mr. Jenkins—he was tough. He taught science and gave special assignments to the "bad" kids. Keith was much worse than Brad, and Louie Carroll was absolutely terrible.

When Louie and Keith were fooling around during one of our microscope lessons in science, Mr. Jenkins made Louie do the urine test. I couldn't believe Mr. Jenkins made us look at urine under a microscope. Disgusting! Even blood wouldn't seem so bad to look at on a slide. But Louie didn't care. He wasn't afraid of anybody. He took forever going to do the "test" and he came back with three cups! The whole class laughed and Louie just said he was glad to help. I couldn't tell if Mr. Jenkins was mad or not, but I think I saw a grin behind his usual stern expression.

Secretly, I was glad Brad wasn't as awful as Louie. One time Louie brought a bottle of wine to school and hid it inside his locker with a package of Dixie cups. He actually tried to sell cups of wine to some of his friends at lunch. Mr. Jenkins caught him in the act and Louie got suspended for two whole weeks.

Mrs. Frazier spoke again. "Class, it's almost November, and the holidays will be here before you know it. So, in keeping with the holiday season, the theme for November is Family Month."

The class groaned, probably thinking the same thing I was. Yeah, families were present at holidays, but what else was there to talk about? What did she mean by a theme for the month?

"Now, give me a break, here. I'm not talking about making construction paper pilgrims or writing a composition on 'What My Family Means To Me.' We're going to go deeper than that."

She retrieved a stack of papers from her desk, crossed to one corner of the room, and began distributing them across the front row for students to pass them back. The hand-outs were yellow. Mrs. Frazier liked yellow. She used it a lot. At least it was better than Mr. Dahl, the funny social studies teacher, who pretended to be the school's biggest MCP—male chauvinist pig. He actually ran off our quizzes on pink and blue paper—pink for the girls and blue for the boys!

The hand-out was a list of assignments for November, Family Month. Some of them were required for everyone;

others were labeled "optional". These weren't for extra credit, as I had learned earlier in the year, but they were *choices*, as Mrs. Frazier called them. She believed in choices on assignments and said they'd make us independent thinkers so we didn't always "follow the crowd". One time I had asked her—then why did we have any standard homework assignments the same as everyone else? 'Some structure,' she had told me, 'is required as a part of living on this planet. Structure is part of our laws and our schools and our jobs. But it's not everything, Cassidy. I want you people to find your own inner-voice, the unique thoughts and ideas and talents that make you who you are. Creativity,' she explained, 'is a skill you have to use every once in a while or you'll get rusty. Creativity comes with exercising choices, being an individual.'

Most of my other teachers didn't believe in choices. I guess they didn't think our creativity needed practice. Mrs. Frazier rattled off the assignments on our handout—family tree, traditions and recipes, heritage collage, and so on. The choices section wasn't so bad. Depending on whether we were artistic or not, we could do a drawing on a family theme, write a story or poem, or even suggest some other project relating to our class discussions over the next few weeks. This was a lot better than diagramming sentences and reading from our English books. At least Mrs. Frazier was trying to make things interesting.

"If you glance at the optional list, you'll see I've listed a few ideas," said Mrs. Frazier. The goal here is to use your imagination to create something meaningful about a family issue or theme. It can be a drawing, poem, or favorite family food you'd like to make and bring in for the class—"

"Could I order a Dominoes pizza?" Keith wanted to know. The class laughed.

Mrs. Frazier smiled. "We're looking for family themes here, Keith. Unless Dominoes is your family business, I think we're looking for a little more imagination."

Keith shrugged.

"How about a song?" asked Linda Beckman, the class flutist.

"Now you're thinking!" said Mrs. Frazier. "As long as the words and the melody express something about a family theme, I'm open to ideas. You've got two weeks to come up with an idea, and your project will be due by the end of the month. That means the earlier you decide, the more time you'll have to work on it."

A special project, I thought. Cooking? Music? Drawing? It's up to us?

Mrs. Frazier walked to the front of the room. She grabbed a piece of chalk and began writing on the board. "Today," she announced, "We're going to start work on one of the required assignments. It is not due for four weeks, but it may take you some time to do a little research and come up with some creative ideas of your own. Again, this is not optional and you just might learn something."

She drew a stick tree and then an outline next to it. "Families can be complicated business," she said. "The general people we all think about when we consider the word 'family' are parents, brothers, sisters, and grandparents. Today, a family member is any care-giver. This includes foster and step-parents, legal guardians, and other people who take care of you. For this assignment, I'm interested in the extended families we all have. Each one of you came from a fairly large group of people, even if you are an only child."

Several of us looked surprised. I noticed Louie doodling on the back of his notebook. Everyone else, however, seemed attentive to what Mrs. Frazier was saying.

"We're going to learn about relationships and how we're all connected to one another. That is just one of the many things that separate people from the rest of creation. We can research, discover, and get to know our broader family tree."

She wrote the words 'cousin', 'aunt', and 'uncle' on the board. "Does anyone know the definition of an aunt?"

Seemed like a pretty basic question to me, so what was she getting at? Brad snickered something about a little bug but Mrs. Frazier didn't hear him.

Lisa's hand went up. "It's the sister of your mother or father," she said primly.

"That's right, Lisa. But it can also be the wife of your mother's brother or of your father's brother. That's an aunt by marriage." The class seemed impressed. Complexity was far more welcome than insulting our intelligence with babyish lessons.

She talked about uncles and cousins. I could tell she meant business. Marcy leaned over to my desk. "Sounds like this is going to be a lot of work," she whispered.

I shrugged. So what? At least it wouldn't be boring. Mrs. Frazier spent some time drawing on the board. She sketched circles and lines and arrows and labeled each object with a "person", such as aunt or uncle, connected to niece, nephew, cousin, and so on.

"Now here is where we get complicated," she smiled. She appeared to be having enormous fun with this. "If two cousins each grow up, get married, and have their own children, what then is the relationship of those children to each other?"

"Little cousins?" one voice offered.

"Well, sort of," answered the teacher. "They are second cousins. But the second cousin's relationship to his mother's or father's cousin—the other parents in this example—is called a 'first cousin, once removed'."

A loud sigh came from the class. This sounded like algebra. Marcy slipped me a note. "If two trains both headed in the opposite direction at noontime, which one had lunch first?" I laughed quietly. Mrs. Frazier had turned back to the board. I couldn't see how she missed the note. That had never stopped her before. I guessed she was too involved in all of the Family Month teaching to make a big deal over a silly note. So what if this was a little tough? Mrs. Frazier seemed to read my thoughts.

"I know what you're thinking," she explained to the class. "This is difficult. It's hard. It's complicated. But you know what? Think of it as challenging. You're going to learn about all of the people in your extended family—the big picture. Trust me, we'll have a good time. It's going to be exciting."

Chapter Three
Peanut Butter Ice Cream?

For the first time in awhile I had the house to myself. Ben had soccer practice until 4:30, and Mom wouldn't be home until 5:30. The afternoon was mine. Though the privacy was great, I was a little scared to be home alone. I chose the chair in the corner—so nobody could sneak up behind me. As I dumped my books on the coffee table, a loud "creak!" made me jump. I hated those noises. Mom always said it was the house "settling", but I couldn't help picturing a creepy guy hiding out in the cellar, or a burglar rummaging through my closet upstairs. I could probably blame this on too many scary news stories on TV. It wasn't from movies since Marcy and I always scare-proofed them first. We asked anyone and everyone if they had seen the movie. Any horror scenes scratched the film from our list. I knew Marcy would never call me a wimp—and besides we shared the fear together.

I made myself think of something else. The freedom of the whole house... I could do anything I wanted. Clicking on the television partly for company, but mostly to distract me from my thoughts, I stood up and headed for the kitchen to grab a snack.

Returning with two oatmeal cookies, I picked up the remote and flipped channels. Just what I thought—nothing on but soaps. What to do now? I could call Marcy, find something to do outside, start my homework... Eyeing my books on the coffee table, I spotted the little heart sticker on my algebra notebook. This made me think of Brad. Today had been a weird day with Brad and me. He talked to me again, so I think we're really getting somewhere. That's twice in the past week.

He made a joke about Marcy's obsession with handwriting analysis. She told him he was overly confident because he wrote so big. He pointed at Marcy and asked me if I thought Marcy should get analyzed since she was being so obnoxious herself. He smiled at me. Those braces looked so clean. I wouldn't mind getting them myself. They made him look really cute. Then again, I'd be the one to get my gum stuck in them. Or even worse—God forbid I ever got to kiss Brad (which would be so amazing)—we might end up like the eighth graders, Bridget and Joel, who accidentally got stuck together one afternoon on the ride home from school. At least everybody *thought* it was an accident. I would never have believed it if I hadn't seen the bus driver trying to force their mouths apart, while the whole bus was laughing. Bridget had been so embarrassed she turned purple and I thought she was going to cry. But Joel just laughed it off and pulled a loose wire straight out of his teeth!

I guess I better not get braces. I would die if that ever happened to me. That would ruin a perfectly amazing kiss from Brad. I don't know what happened to Bridget and Joel after that but I don't think they are going out anymore.

After rifling through my books, I found my English notebook. Lots of thinking to do about these Family Month projects. I needed some really original ideas for a project. Something big that no one else was going to do. Not just some stupid collage or drawing thing. I needed a fantastic idea.

This project was major, and I really wanted to impress Mrs. Frazier. She got so excited about her freedom-project style of teaching where we got a lot of say in our work, and I didn't want her to think I couldn't handle the responsibility. I was mature enough, just not creative enough—yet. Hoping that the spark of imagination would strike soon, I decided to talk to Dad this weekend.

A busy account executive for an ad firm, he was great at these things. Maybe he could help me with some ideas. Just a little input might get my thoughts flowing and then I'd be on my way.

The doorbell rang. I looked at my watch. Quarter past three—who could it be? I checked the peephole on tiptoe and saw Josh. What was he doing here? I opened the door and let him in.

"Hi Cass. How's it going?"

"Good," I said without expression.

"I know your Mom's not home from work yet, but I came to drop this off."

"Drop what off?"

"It's her ticket for the play we're going to this Friday night. I have to stay late for parent-teacher conferences so I'll have to meet your Mom there and she needs her ticket to get in. Can you give it to her?"

"Sure. What play are you going to see?"

"Oh, it's a comedy called <u>Private Lives</u>. Noel Coward. His stuff is really funny. I bet you'd like it."

"Really?" I had never been to a grown-up play.

"Maybe I'll take you sometime if you'd like."

"Okay." I shrugged, hiding my enthusiasm a little.

Not wanting to be rude for Mom's sake, I decided to invite him in. "Do you want a drink or something? I'm just doing some homework."

"Well, I should probably be correcting papers for my class but I've got a few minutes." He removed his jacket and followed me into the kitchen.

"It's okay, I'll get it." He grabbed a Pepsi bottle and poured himself a cup and then one for me.

I didn't want Pepsi. I was into clear soda—a "phase" as Mom would call it. All the cola drinks were out and I only wanted ginger ale and Sprite and 7-Up. Nice or not, Josh was always doing stuff like that, and it drove me crazy. He didn't ask what I wanted. He just assumed I wanted the same thing he did.

Annoyed, I said "You can have mine," and pushed the cup back toward him. "I don't really like Pepsi anymore. I'll just get some ginger ale and you can have my drink when you're done with yours."

I didn't look at him. This was the first time I had said something to undo what he just did. I was afraid he'd get mad if I spoke up.

He didn't. "Oh. I didn't know that. Ginger ale, huh?" He shrugged. "Sorry."

"That's okay." I took my drink to the living room and sat on the couch. Josh joined me and put his feet up on the table. Mom's table. He didn't have his big muddy boots on this time but still, they were shoes and Mom hated shoes on the coffee table. She said they scratched the surface and made digs in the wood. I watched his feet and kept eyeing the table for damage.

Dad had never put his feet up on that table. I wondered what Mom would do if she saw Josh just sitting there with his two Pepsi drinks and his feet up on the table with his shoes on. I didn't say anything to Josh. I hoped he'd get the hint with my laser stare.

He didn't. At least I don't think he knew. He just kept talking to me. Maybe he knew I was irritated with him. I wasn't even sure why I felt so mean.

"So Cass, how's school?"

"Fine."

"You like all your teachers this year?"

"They're okay."

"Nobody awesome like me, huh?" He laughed.

I laughed a little too. "No." He probably would be a good teacher to have since he seemed to be in such a good mood all the time. That would be a change. Most of my teachers yelled—or at least grouched a lot.

Josh pointed to the television. "Aw, Ben would hate missing this," he laughed. A peanut butter commercial was on and some nuts were dancing all over the television.

"Yeah, he loves this one." He was right. Ben loved musical commercials the best and this peanut butter one was one of his favorites.

Josh swung his feet off the table and stood up. "Hey!" he said loudly. "I've got an idea. You wanna learn how to make peanut butter ice cream?"

"How to make ice cream? You mean like with an ice cream maker?"

"No—easier than that. Tell you what. Let's check the freezer and see if we have all the good old ingredients to mix us up a batch."

I followed him into the kitchen. He pulled out bowls and spoons and spread everything all over the counter. We had the stuff he said we needed. Vanilla ice cream, peanut butter, a banana to squish up on top. He even took out a jar of honey to make the ice cream extra sticky.

Josh decided I would be in charge of the biggest bowl. He piled mounds of vanilla ice cream into our largest mixing bowl—using almost the entire box. We were going to make a lot of ice cream.

"Can I stir in the peanut butter?" I asked him, looking for direction. The vanilla ice cream was still cold and it made the peanut butter clot and stick in a giant lump in the center. I thought about Josh as I stirred. Feeling guilty about my irritation with him earlier, I decided to try harder. Maybe Mom was right. Maybe he wasn't trying to be my Dad.

"Yup. Just use a really big spoon or else you'll drown in the bowl and you'll get peanut butter up to your elbows."

"Okay. How much should I use?" The jar was almost half-full.

"As much as you want. You like peanut butter a whole lot?"

I nodded.

"Then use the whole thing," he laughed. "We'll just find one of your Mom's Tupperware containers and save it all in there when we're done."

He made me forget about the shoes on the coffee table and the Pepsi. This was great! We made ice cream—almost from scratch. We made a mess and the honey and peanut butter and banana made sticky globs all over me, the counter, the floor, and even Josh—since he was in charge of the honey—but we had a blast.

After the ice cream was totally made and squished into two big Tupperware containers in the freezer, we decided to fix everything before Mom got home. Then we could eat the ice cream in peace and nobody would get in trouble.

Feeling more relaxed as we dragged out sponges and a mop to clean up the ice cream mess, I decided to talk to him about the marriage situation. "Josh? Did you ever want kids of your own?"

He looked up from the mop, his expression a bit surprised. "Well, I thought I did, but it just hasn't worked out that way. I'm getting a bit of a late start with your Mom and I'm not sure if she wants any more children right now. We'll have to see."

I paused, deciding if I should say any more. "I mean, does it bother you that you're moving in with us and marrying Mom, but you're not our real Dad?" I scrubbed the counter harder, focusing on a little glob of honey that stuck to the surface, so I wouldn't have to look at him. When the silence seemed a bit too long, I looked up and saw that he was smiling at me.

His expression then grew more serious. "No, Cassie, I would never try to be your father. Nobody can replace your Dad."

Now I felt a little silly for asking. Of course he knew this already. What was I thinking? I inspected the counter again.

The honey glob came loose and I sponged the rest of the countertop, using extra lemon cleanser so the whole kitchen smelled good. He was busy mopping the floor.

"I just love your mother and you guys so much that I want to be a part of the family. It doesn't matter if I'm a step-father or any other name you call it." He rinsed the mop and swirled it again in the soapy bucket. "I'll be with you and we can share good times and be a part of each other's lives. That's what a family is. It's made up of love and time together. Wouldn't you agree?" He looked over at me. This time I felt all right to look at him, no longer embarrassed.

I nodded. "Definitely. I just wondered…"

He looked concerned. "Cassie," he began, "Are you okay about your Mom and me getting married?"

Wondering if Mom had said anything, I shrugged and said weakly "I guess..." trying to convince myself more than him."It's just a little strange for us I guess."

"Yeah, I know what you mean. It'll be an adjustment for me too—living with two ladies in the house and a feisty little kid, having to share all my great toys, never getting to watch what I want on television..."

"Hey!" I laughed. "No way... *We're* the ones who have to share..."

"I'm only kidding!" he chuckled. "Seriously, it'll be great being together. And you know, I'm always here if you ever need to talk."

"Thanks," I said, believing him. "That means a lot."

After he left, I thought about the afternoon. Josh had made it fun. I didn't even miss my afternoon of having the house to myself. Ben was jealous when he found out we actually made our own ice cream, but he felt better when we shared the bounty. This was our time today, just Josh and me. And as far as privacy and ruling the house for a few hours was concerned, this was much, much better.

Chapter Four
Handwriting Analysis

Miss Storrigan waddled her way up and down the aisles of

our study hall, her gaze shifting over the tops of our desks like

a supermarket scanner. Marcy and I got to sit side by side in

this class—if you could call study hall a class—as long as we

didn't disturb anybody too much. "Too much" was the key

with Miss Storrigan. She was proper and almost always

slightly disapproving of all the students, but she let us talk—

quietly—in study hall. I think the only reason she marched up

and down the rows of our desks is to guard against anyone

copying homework and of course, to check for gum. She was amazing with that wastebasket. All a kid had to do was swallow funny or make the slightest click of a squashed bubble and the gum was history. Miss Storrigan had the basket out and in front of the kid before anyone knew somebody had been busted. What's more, she had a penalty for gum chewing—or should I say—gum *catching*. Anybody caught chewing gum in her class paid a 50¢ charge—a real fee—due that day or very soon after. I've heard people say she actually sent bills and kept track if a student didn't pay up. She said all the money went to charity—for children who have never seen gum, let alone chewed it in school. I believed her. It certainly didn't go to her clothes. I'd seen pictures of Mom and Dad in clothes like that in the 1970s.

Marcy nudged me in the arm as I scribbled my name on the paper.

"No, Cass—you have to write more than one word. Try something with a lot of vowels so I can see your 'a's and 'o's."

"My 'a's and 'o's? What's so special about my 'a's and 'o's?" Marcy's mother took classes for everything. Her latest kick was handwriting analysis and she had shown Marcy a few tricks.

"You'll see," she said mysteriously. I wrote "A quick brown fox jumps over the lazy dog" on the paper. I remembered that sentence from fourth grade penmanship. It used every letter in the alphabet.

Marcy was impressed. "Cool," she said. "Now let me look this over."

She was quiet for a few minutes while she looked over my writing, intently studying the letters. I didn't know what to expect, but it was fun doing this analysis thing anyway. I thought about what Mrs. Frazier had said in class this morning. She had talked some more about Family Month and it would definitely be a big deal. I had to come up with something fantastic. If I decided to cook something, I could talk to Mom about our German ancestry. I could make red cabbage with raisins. Then again, Louie would probably make some nasty comment about cabbage. Or strudel. I could make apple strudel, with tons and tons of cinnamon glaze like Mom always made. Maybe I could write a poem with a picture to match, like those watercolors with the black writing over them we did last spring in art class. I wanted it to be special, my own. I wanted my own voice to come through, just like Mrs. Frazier had said.

"Cass, I'm done," said Marcy. "Are you ready?"

I wasn't ready. I was on a roll with this project thing. So much to think about—so little time. I wasn't much in the mood for talking.

"I guess so."

"Well, I'll write this out for you," said Marcy with a professional sound in her voice, "but we'll just go over it for now."

I guessed her mother must have practiced on Marcy. I wondered if this would be a new career for Mrs. Nickerson. I pictured distraught, but well-dressed clients being escorted into Marcy's home after supper—the same as the manicure clients and eager tarot card followers.

"You have a right slant to your writing," said Marcy. "It's not straight up and down, which would mean you are very logical and it's not pointing to the left—which can mean confusion and some weird stuff."

"Like what?" I wanted to know.

44

"I don't know. My mother just said it was really weird and she was going to learn about it in her next class."

"Oh."

She continued. "So, as I was saying, your writing slants to the right—which means you're emotional. As my mother explained it, 'you're ruled by the heart and not your head'."

I was insulted. "So what does that mean—I'm dumb?"

"No," she laughed. "It means you're—*sensitive*. Treat it as a compliment. Maybe you're a hopeless romantic. I bet Brad would appreciate that."

"Shut up!" I whisper-yelled, looking up at Miss Storrigan. She stared back at me over her glasses. I tried to smile.

"Just kidding, Cass. Gosh!" said Marcy. "Can't take a joke, now can you?"

"I can take plenty of jokes. I just think I'm both."

"Both what?"

"Ruled by the heart and the head. Can't a person have thoughts and feelings and just do whatever?"

"Sure," she shrugged.

Now I wanted to know more. "What else?"

"Well, lucky for me, your 'a's and 'o's are closed tight—no gaps here."

"What does that mean?"

"It means you're not a blabber-mouth. You can keep a secret, trustworthy."

I nodded, proud of this. "Sure."

"And, based on today's sample," she added, sounding definitely like a teacher. "You are a very positive and optimistic person."

"Based on what?"

"Your 't's."

"My 't's?" I waited for an explanation.

"You cross your 't's with a slight upswing. Like a seesaw, the line goes up a little from left to right. That's a good mood, a positive person. Down would mean negative, a pessimist like my Dad—or maybe even your Dad."

I had no response to this. I wasn't sure what my Dad was— except not around me very much lately.

"Hey!" said Marcy. "I almost forgot—no pun intended. You're not forgetful."

"I'm not?"

"No. You don't forget to cross your 't's and dot your 'i's. My Mom said that's a sure sign of a forgetful person."

***

I left study hall in a good mood. I was beginning to get some ideas for Family Month. I was positive and trustworthy and not forgetful. So what if I was emotional? That just meant I had feelings. That was a good thing. I would never be cold or uncaring. It wasn't in my personality—or in my penmanship.

I noticed Mrs. Frazier's door was open after the bell rang and most of the kids had cleared out. Ben would be waiting if I didn't hurry up and get home, but I wanted to stop by and ask her something. She had talked a lot about "care-givers" lately, and I just wanted to ask how they fit into the mandatory family tree assignment.

She was sitting at her desk, reading.

I knocked and stood in the doorway. "Mrs. Frazier?"

"Hello, Cassidy."

"Hi. I just wanted to ask you something. It'll only take a minute."

"Take all the time you need, I'm always here late on Wednesdays for my students. Do you need help with something?"

"Well, not like teaching help exactly. I just need some advice."

"Sure," she said. "I'm listening."

"Well, you know when you were talking about care-givers in class—and how families come in all shapes and sizes?"

"Yes."

"Well, where do you put an extra care-giver if you already have two real parents?"

"You mean biological parents?"

"Yes."

"Well, you can add anyone in to your family tree that you consider part of your upbringing, part of your life."

"I can?"

She smiled. "Sure, you can. It's your tree. You can make as many branches as you want. The key is to understand the relationships, how everybody fits together. The people in your life are like a wonderful puzzle. Each person touches your life in some special way. But not all of our "family" members are related biologically."

I didn't say anything, but my face must have looked relieved.

She continued. "There are adoptive parents and foster parents and stepbrothers and stepsisters, and all sorts of people that can be a guardian or a very close friend."

"Okay, so I can include my other special care-givers then. Does it matter where I put them on my tree?"

"No, that's up to you, Cassidy. Of course, we're all going to learn the relationships among uncles and aunts and cousins and grandparents. It's important to know how people are connected. But that's just the beginning. The real meaning is finding out about the people who have helped you become the person you are."

"Thanks, Mrs. Frazier. You've helped me a lot." I turned to leave the room and was sure now that if I didn't jog all the way home, Ben would be waiting on the front step, without his key. He never remembered. He never really had to. I always made sure I got there first. Come to think of it, he probably didn't dot his 'i's or cross his 't's either.

"Cassidy?"

I turned quickly before heading out the door.

"I'm here anytime you need to talk."

"Thanks. Bye, Mrs. Frazier."

Chapter Five
Taking Charge

I got home just as Ben was making his way up the front

walk. He didn't even look worried that I didn't meet him at the

bus stop at the end of our street. He was such a funny kid—

totally opposite of me. He never seemed to panic until he

absolutely knew there was trouble. Marcy says that's because

he's an Aries. Likes to be in charge, but somehow laid back at

the same time. Like the time he punched Billy Kearney in the

stomach when Billy pushed him off the top of the slide. He

just told me matter-of-factly what happened that day after he

51

got home and he didn't cry or anything. He must have known he'd be in trouble when Mom found out. Mom had told him no more fights, but this time nobody saw and Billy had deserved it. He was always picking on Ben. I knew it and I think Mom knew it, but she had never told Ben it was okay to hit anybody who picks on you. Besides, Mrs. Kearney had called Mom and told her it was obvious a working mother couldn't discipline her kid and Ben was proof. That made Mom mad at first but later I think she was sad because she kept asking me if she was doing a good job raising us. That was right after Dad left.

"Hey, Ben," I said as I reached for my house key. "How was school?"

"Good. We played dodge ball in gym today. It took a long time to get me out." He beamed. The dodge ball champion.

"That's great! Did you win this time?"

"No. There were three kids left when the bell rang. The teacher called it a tie."

"Oh. Do you have any homework you have to do?"

"Only a little. Just some cursive writing thing and this page about hurricanes and tornadoes. We learned about them at school today."

"Cool. You learned about storms today? Did you do that soda bottle thing where the water fizzes up and swirls around just like a real tornado?"

"Yeah, that was fun. We even put in some blue food coloring so the water looked an ocean tornado. And you know what?"

"What?"

"We learned about hurricanes and they have an eye, you know. But it's not a real eye." He squinted at me, trying to make one eye wink, then holding one closed with his finger. He always had trouble winking without finger cheating.

"Yeah? What do you know about the eye?"

"My teacher said it's like a quiet place in the middle of the storm. A space where nothing really happens until the storm moves on and it gets windy and rainy again."

"That's really cool, Ben." I imagined a nothing place and wondered why it was called an eye.

We weren't inside more than a minute before Ben had thrown his jacket on the floor, tossed his workbooks on the kitchen table, and flicked on the television. He found cartoons before I had my coat off.

"Ben, wait a minute. Your jacket?" I pointed to the pile on the floor.

"Oh. I forgot." He jumped up from his place in front of the TV and threw the jacket over the railing in the hall. It wasn't his room but it was sort of hung up, so I let it go. Mom made less of a big deal over coats if they were at least hung up—and a railing was sort of hung up. At least it wasn't on the floor.

"Don't forget, Ben! Mom said you have to set the table," I called into the next room. "Bossy," was what Ben sometimes called me on the days I was "in charge". I hated that word. It was such a snotty word and one that especially got to me if somebody used it to describe me. Funny how some days I really liked feeling important and all grown-up, managing things. Whenever I got home from school, there were always a ton of things to do. There was the job of cleaning up any mess leftover from the morning of Ben and me rushing to school, making sure Ben didn't fill up on too much junk food, and both of us doing our homework. Sometimes I even helped start dinner. I wasn't crazy about the work, but I liked doing grown-up things and helping Mom out since she started working again.

Sometimes it wasn't much fun being in charge. It would be cool to be like Marcy, who didn't have any chores except to make her bed and feed her two fish that she named Glitz and Glamour. She would never name a goldfish "Goldie" or a cat "Fluffy". It's not that she especially hated names like that. They just didn't occur to her. Her family had more money than mine and Mrs. Montgomery had hired a cleaning lady to come in two afternoons a week. I didn't want the money or the things, really. It was her freedom. Marcy acted grown-up a lot of the time, but she didn't have to. Nobody expected her to help out or even to babysit her little sister Emily. Of course, Emily was almost ten and she didn't have any rules either. She went through this stage where she would wear only yellow tops and blue jeans. Nobody knows why. Most moms would just insist their kids change their outfits so it didn't look like they were wearing the same thing every day. Not Mrs. Montgomery. She actually went out and bought a few more yellow sweatshirts and even dyed a perfectly good white sweater yellow because Emily wouldn't wear it otherwise. Mrs. Montgomery never seemed to make a big deal about homework getting done or what her kids snacked on before dinner. She seemed so mellow most of the time. It was a wonder Marcy ever did her homework. She must be a self-starter, the same term Mom called me sometimes when I got all of my homework done and still ran things at home after school.

I stood in the middle of the kitchen and surveyed the room around me. The room looked like spring. Oak cabinets lined two walls of the room and soft creamy wallpaper with tiny yellow daisies covered the rest of the kitchen. The long kitchen counters were a cheerful yellow, with matching lace curtains framing the window over the sink. I had just finished wiping the counters and tabletops clean and spraying the front of the stove and dishwasher. The room smelled clean and lemony, and I hated to drag out the dinner stuff and mess everything up.

I grabbed a pencil from the memo board on the wall and crossed kitchen clean-up and vacuuming from Mom's list. I caught sight of a note on the fridge. After pulling it from its smiley face magnet, I read it out loud. "Cassie, please make salad. Be home by 5:30. Love, Mom." Sighing to nobody, I opened the refrigerator, and jimmied the crisper door to get it open. It always seemed to catch on one side. I pulled out a bag of carrots, a stalk of celery, and a head of lettuce from the drawer. Leaving the drawer open, I scooted over to the sink, and dumped the vegetables on the counter. I went back for the tomatoes, grabbing four and slamming the fridge door shut. Ben and I loved tomatoes. Under the cabinet, I found a Tupperware bowl big enough to hold the salad. It took forever to sort through a stack of lids until I found the large yellow one that matched the bowl.

The cutting board was under the microwave on the second shelf of the cart. It was shaped like Mickey Mouse's head, and it always reminded me of our trip to Disney World when I was in the third grade. Four years ago and it seemed like forever. Ben was in pre-school then and didn't remember much. He just talked about the fireworks and the parade with all of the lights. The parade was a good memory—with lots of balloons and songs and crowds of people trying to see Mickey and all of his friends. The fireworks were scary because they were loud and sounded like gunfire. Plus it was dark. Ben still didn't like the dark. Even now, he had a little baseball night light that Mom kept on when he went to bed.

I pulled the colander from the cabinet and rinsed the tomatoes first. "Ben!" I yelled into the family room. "Come on, I need you to set the table now. Mom's gonna be home soon."

"In a minute," he called back. "Sponge Bob is almost over." I didn't know whether to be "bossy" and tell him to come now or to laugh at his taste in TV shows.

I glanced at the kitchen clock. It was ten past five. Mom should be home in about 20 minutes. His show had just started! I had to be bossy this time.

"On the commercial, Ben. It can't wait 'til your show is over. Mom will be home by then."

"Okay, okay," I heard him mumble. "On the commercial." There was a pause, then "It just better not be a good commercial".

I couldn't help but laugh. Marcy called Ben the little TV addict. For a nine year-old, it was amazing how he could watch almost anything and look really interested, as if the TV were a magnet sucking him into every show, every commercial. Setting the table didn't take that long. It could wait a few minutes until a commercial. I smiled—being in charge didn't always mean bossy.

I peeled the carrots and sliced them into little sticks, and then did the celery. The lettuce was easy, just broken up by hand and crunched into the bowl. I didn't do much tossing, but the vegetables were pretty mixed up, so I quit there. While I washed my hands, I looked out the window over the sink. It was early November and the sky had already darkened to a deep purple-blue. The moon was almost full, and glowed like a shiny gold coin in the dark sky. Autumn felt like magic with the cool nights and colored leaves, but I couldn't stand the way it got dark so early. It made things feel a little more lonely until Mom came home. The lonely feeling reminded me of Dad. It had been almost a year now and I still missed him living here. The only thing I *didn't* miss was the fighting. The last one had been the worst...

I had seen the whole thing from the stairs and couldn't stop crying. Mom was hysterical and Dad kept yelling. Mom had said she couldn't take it anymore but I never understood the whole thing. I knew they yelled a lot. They said "responsibility" during almost every fight, and then Dad would curse and say "Damn it, Ellen" as if Mom were a little girl who had just spilled some milk on a brand new carpet. I couldn't stand the screaming. The worst part was the way they would wait until they thought I was asleep to start talking. It always began that way—talking. Muffled sounds would rise and fall from beneath the floor of my bedroom, but I could never make out the words. Sometimes it would sound like laughter or Dad sounding excited about something, but then it would turn into yelling and I could never tell if Mom was angry with Dad or if Dad was mad at Mom.

I didn't know that fight would be the last. They had yelled before and things always seemed to calm down by breakfast the next day. This time was different. Dad didn't stop yelling and Mom didn't give in either. Then he left. Didn't even take his jacket—just grabbed his keys from the kitchen table and slammed the door. That was in January. Dad moved out back then.

"Keeyah!" Ben cheered with a karate leap into the kitchen. I couldn't believe he actually came in on the commercial. Impressive. No reminders needed this time.

"Boring commercial?" I asked him when he scuffed over to the counter and hoisted himself up to get the dishes.

"Just some dopey hair thing," he said. I peeked around the corner to see the familiar face of the fake hair guy selling toupees. Ben hated "talking" commercials. He liked music the best—especially candy and gum commercials or the cool songs they made up for soda commercials.

I watched him yank the forks from the drawer and slap one down at each place setting on the table—three people, still a little sad without Dad. I watched him pull down three drinking glasses and leave the place at the far end of the table empty. It was an oak rectangular table, and Mom and Dad had always sat at the long ends while he and I sat on either side. Ben said nothing while he finished setting the table. I wondered if he ever wished Dad still lived here.

Chapter Six
Family Mouth

Mom came in at supper time and I helped her with the chop suey so we could talk. I told her all about Marcy's mother taking handwriting analysis and what she said about my writing slanting to the right.

"Mom, do you think I'm too emotional?"

"Honey, of course you're emotional. Everybody has emotions to some degree." She smiled. "But I think you take after me. Being emotional doesn't mean anything bad. It just means you're sensitive to people's feelings. That's a good thing."

"So you don't think I get too upset over things that are bad, do you?"

"Cassidy, what are you talking about?"

"About Dad. Not seeing us that much lately. He always cancels out on me and Ben because of work. Do you think I shouldn't get angry at him?"

"Well, it's funny you should ask. First—no, I don't think you have been too upset. You've had good reasons to be angry with your father. I was upset with him too. You and Ben are his children, even if he doesn't live here anymore. But, you'll get another chance to talk to him. This weekend—if you want."

"What's this weekend?"

"He called me at work today, this morning. He said he was thinking about you and he wanted to take you and Ben out on Saturday. Something about bowling and a movie. His schedule has calmed down and he wants to get back to seeing you guys every other Saturday."

"He does?" I considered this. Maybe he missed us. Good. He should feel a little bad about not coming to visit us that much lately. I gave Mom her favorite answer she usually told us when we wanted to do something. "We'll see."

Satisfied with this, she changed the subject. "What else happened today?" she asked, pulling a bag of mixed vegetables from the freezer. It was the good kind. No cauliflower in this one.

"Do you know what month it is?" I quizzed Mom.

"It's November," she paused, waiting for a clarification to the strange question.

"Nope. It's Family Month. According to Mrs. Frazier, in English class." I was glad to get a chance to talk to Mom, since I hadn't mentioned the projects the other day.

Mom smiled. She liked Mrs. Frazier. Everybody liked her.

"We're doing a family tree and learning about relatives and relationships and first cousins once removed—a whole bunch of things. And the best part is we have to think up something creative for a special project—each one of us gets to do something original."

"Any ideas about what you want to do?"

"Well I have too many, actually. I could get your recipe for apple strudel and make some to bring in for the class as part of my German ancestry. Or I could make a collage of pictures with some kind of family theme. Or write a poem or draw something, or..."

"Whoa!" Mom laughed. "Sounds like you're really looking forward to this!"

"I am."

"Well, I'm glad. It's nice to see you so enthusiastic about something. You let me know if you need any help, okay?"

"Okay, I will. I mean, I'm sure I'll need some, but I don't know what yet. But we only have up to two weeks to decide so I better get busy thinking."

***

Later that night, I thought about what Mom had said in the kitchen. Josh was great. But I still missed Dad. The thought of seeing him Saturday made me realize how much I had missed him over the past few weeks. I decided to give him a call. I went to use Mom's phone in her bedroom and dialed his new home number. Busy. I decided to call Marcy and try him again later.

Chapter Seven
Making Dad Plans

I reached Marcy on the first try. She always answered the phone. You'd think it was her own private number.

"Hey—what's up?" I said as I marched around my mother's room. I was hoping for my own phone on my thirteenth birthday, but until then Mom gave me permission to use hers. I wandered around Mom's bedroom with the phone until I found myself in front of her dresser. Hers was the only non-cordless phone in the house because she loved the antique-looking style, but the extra long cord made it possible to walk all over the room.

The huge, three-paneled mirror made me look taller than I really was. I loved Mom's things. She had beautiful perfume bottles and sparkly glass figurines on her bureau. Everything was dainty and lacey. The room smelled soft like Mom, a mixture of perfume and potpourri.

"Nothing much. Still haven't finished my homework yet. Good TV on tonight, though."

"Well you better hurry up then," I teased, knowing full well my bedtime was two hours before Marcy's. She told me once that she often fell asleep on the couch in her family room because she just stayed up until she got too tired to move. Her parents didn't make rules like my Mom. Even during sleepovers, her Mom never even told us to get to bed by a certain time. Didn't she know mothers are always supposed to tell you a time, even if they know you'll talk all night 'cause your friends are over?

"I will. Hey, have you started your tree yet?"

"Yeah, I've thought about it a little." I wasn't sure if this was a lie since I was thinking about it a lot. But I hadn't actually done any work on it yet.

"What are you making the tree out of?"

"Why?"

"Well you know how she said we should be creative? Well I'm doing mine out of pipe cleaners so the whole thing is flexible—it can move and bend. Like those bonsai trees you can cut into shape that we did in science. Only mine's just bendable into different shapes."

"Cool!" This made my environmental idea feel boring.

"So do you know yet what your tree'll be made of?"

"Well I was thinking 'natural'. The whole thing will be like a real tree, only miniature. I can use my Mom's glue gun to glue sticks and leaves together to make it look real."

"Awesome. Almost as good as my idea," she laughed.

"No you mean *better* than your idea," I insisted.

"No way. At best you get a tie."

"You sound like my little brother. He was bummed about his dodge ball game being a tie today. He likes to win."

"Who doesn't?"

69

"I gotta go. I have to call my father back. We might be doing something Saturday."

"This is good, right? You miss him?"

I shrugged and then felt silly since she couldn't see me anyway. "Yeah, it's good. I miss him. I just feel funny sometimes, you know? Like half-mad and half-psyched. We have a good time, it's just I hate the way he cancels a lot—like we're not important."

"Yeah. I know what you mean. Not about being separated but about canceling. My Dad's always missing things even though he still lives with us. He travels a lot. Dads are always too busy."

"I know. I'll see you tomorrow. Good luck with the pipe cleaners!"

"You too. Bye!"

I hung up the phone and returned to Mom's dresser before leaving the room. There was a picture of Ben and me on top of her jewelry box, another one of me as a baby, and a new one of Josh. He was smiling, or maybe laughing. He was wearing his old blue sweatshirt and a baseball cap. His shirt was all wet because that was the day a few weeks ago when we had all washed the cars and had a hose fight afterwards. Every one of us got soaked. He was first. Even Mom got wet and she had tried really hard to stay out of the way until we were done. She had said she was making lunch but I think she just didn't want to get soaked. Ben loved it. He said it beat all of his watergun fights because the hose got you drenched so much quicker. Josh chased him with the hose to get even.

I switched Mom's light off and went back to my room. I thought about what kind of phone I wanted. Marcy had a funny Garfield one, all orange, with eyes that opened and closed when you picked up the receiver. Mom's was a white fancy French-style phone, with gold rings over the numbers. Maybe I'd get one of the cordless fluorescent ones with the glow-in-the-dark numbers. Then I could call Marcy after my bedtime in the dark. That would be cool.

I pulled out some of the sticks I had gathered for my family tree this afternoon (I guess I had done a little work on the project after all), and spread them out on the floor. I hadn't asked for the glue gun yet so I just did some pre-arranging. The few leaves I had were all brown and crunchy since it was fall, so I might have to use pine needles instead. I could make

71

it an evergreen tree. That would fit even better anyway since families are supposed to last and evergreens stay the same all year round.

I hadn't made the labels yet. I had to find something "natural". My list of names included Mom, and Ben, Gramma and Grampa, and Dad and Uncle Jim and Aunt Laurie, plus my five-year-old cousin Betsy and 15-year-old cousin Greg. This was going to be a bigger tree than I had thought. I'd definitely need more branches and something real solid to use as a base so the tree wouldn't fall over.

Then there was Josh. He was sort of family. Maybe even a "care-giver" like Mrs. Frazier said. He was going to be tough. I scribbled his name and Dad's and Mom's and Ben's on some scrap paper and tore it into little pieces with one name on each piece. I laid out my branches and put some labels next to the branches. Gramma and Grampa would go at the top off to one side and on the other side... Oh, I forgot Nana Peterson. She'd have to go opposite Gramma and Grampa and I'd have to ask Mom what Dad's father's name was again. He died before I was born and I couldn't remember the name sometimes. I knew it began with an "A" and was kind of a strange name—

like Anton or Alwin or Alonzo... That was it! Alonzo! Out loud I said, "Alonzo, let's make you a label right now". I scribbled his name on a little piece of paper and put him next to Nana Peterson.

Dad and Mom were next. I'd put them side by side...but what about the divorce? I couldn't glue them together like Gramma and Grampa. Or even Alonzo and Nana Peterson. At least he was dead and they were still married so that didn't count. But Dad had left. So what was I supposed to do? I decided to move him a little over so he'd have a few pine needles between him and Mom. And Ben, he'd go under Mom, next to me, but a little lower since he's the baby.

And Josh... I stared at his little piece of paper. I put him next to Mom. That pushed Dad too far off the branch and he fell off. I put him under Mom, next to Ben and me. But then he looked like another kid. If I moved him up top he looked old like Gramma and Grampa. This was giving me a headache. I looked at the clock. It was almost 9:00 and I was getting tired. Josh would have to wait until later. I guessed he wouldn't mind. For now I put him behind Mom. Nobody would know he was there because Mom's name was in front.

Maybe I'd get a bigger branch. Anyway, thank goodness this wasn't due for a few more days. I needed more branches anyway. And pine needles—lots of pine needles.

The tree made me think of Dad. I decided to give him one more try. Bowling would be fun on Saturday. I sneaked back into Mom's room because it was getting late and I should at least be getting ready for bed by now. I left the light off since the hall light was enough to get to the phone.

This time, Dad's line wasn't busy.

"Hi, Dad? It's me, Cassie."

"Hello, Cassie. Is everything all right?"

He sounded a little tired. I hoped I didn't wake him up. "Fine, Dad. I just called about Saturday. Mom said you wanted to take Ben and me out for the day."

"Yes, if that's all right with you, I thought we'd go bowling. You guys have such a good time."

"Yeah, and maybe we can get sundaes again. The winner pays."

He laughed. Dad always won. Ben and I didn't care though. As long as we got bumpers in the alley like the little kids, we were happy. This way the ball could zigzag all over the place and still get us a strike since the gutters were blocked. Dad didn't like us wanting bumpers but we always voted and he lost. Plus he didn't bowl gutters anyway so they didn't mess up his score.

"Sounds good. I'll pick you guys up around 10:00."

"Okay, see you then. Bye, Dad."

I hung up the phone. I was a little surprised to find I didn't feel so sad about Dad anymore. Not even mad. Bowling would be great this weekend. Plus maybe we could talk and try to see him more. He sounded like he really wanted to go. That made all the difference. I'd tell Ben in the morning. He'd be psyched.

I changed into my pajamas without brushing my teeth. I was in a good mood but it was late and I didn't feel like walking all the way down the hall to the bathroom. I slipped into bed and felt happier than I did all day. Things were starting to fit. I was so tired I fell asleep within seconds.

Chapter Eight
Bowling Bumpers

Dad was late, so we only got to the bowling alley a little
before lunch time. We could hear the smack of the pins and
the thump-thump of the balls from out in the parking lot.
When we got inside it was smoky already and the place was
crowded with kids and Moms and Dads. It smelled of sweat
and cigars and stale pretzels. Saturday mornings were good
because Dad said there weren't any leagues. Ben got to the
counter first and ordered shoes.

"Size two," he said to the man with the cigar behind the counter. Ben had such little feet.

"Could I have a five and a half?" I asked.

"That's a two, and a five and a half. You sir?" He eyed my father.

"I have my own shoes, thank you."

He plopped Ben's and my shoes on the counter. "That'll be $3.00 for the shoes."

Dad paid him and the man looked for an open lane. There were two. Number fourteen was open and down the little kids' end was lane number five. "Let's see, lane number fourteen?" He handed my father a score sheet and pencil.

"Got any with bumpers?" Ben interrupted. The man looked at us and then over to Dad.

"You know, the little blue things," Ben explained.

"Yeah, but those are for the little kids. Do you really want bumpers?"

Ben nodded. "Yes, we do."

I backed him up. "The game's much more fun that way."

The man shrugged. My father looked away. Ben and I fought for the scorekeeper job as we made our way to lane number five. The seats on either side of us were filled with preschoolers' jackets and sneakers and somebody's Mom kept score in each of the lanes. One side looked like a birthday party, where there were presents on the chairs and a few kids were playing with toy horns.

"Did we embarrass you, Dad?" I nudged him in the arm.

He shrugged. "A little. You kids know how I feel about bumpers at your age. Do we honestly need these things to have fun?"

"Yes!" Ben and I cheered in unison.

That made Dad smile. He knew we had won again. Two out of three and as long as Ben and I stuck together we'd keep the bumpers.

Ben's shoes looked like miniature versions of Dad's even though Dad's were new and much nicer. They were both blue and grey with a stripe down the middle. Mine looked like Christmas shoes with red and green patches all over them. They were all scuffed up and kind of ugly but it was still fun wearing somebody else's shoes. I liked the way they slid across the wooden floor of the bowling lanes. It was a little like skating but with no blades.

Ben liked to be in charge of the computer score screen. He put Dad first, then himself, and then me. We all gave ourselves one practice turn that didn't count. I didn't know if the leagues did it that way but that was one rule we all agreed on. The special add-on rule that I made up started a few months ago when I bowled a nine on my practice and a two on my first real turn. This rule allows the bowler to pick the best of the first two turns if the practice score is really good. Ben liked this one. Dad didn't say. But he hadn't used this rule yet. Dad was a really good bowler. Ben liked looking at the little cartoons dance across the screen—especially whenever anybody got a spare or strike. He didn't get to see the cartoons much when he and I bowled, but at least we didn't get zeroes. It's pretty tough to get a zero with a bumper in each gutter. The bumpers knock almost every ball toward the middle of the pins so you always get *something* down.

Dad took his practice and bowled a spare. Ben only got a five so it was good that one didn't count.

"Ben, you walk three steps starting out on your left," Dad said. He moved up to show Ben. "See? One, two, three. Now bend and release the ball off the tips of your fingers."

"Like this?" Ben tried to mimic Dad's broad stride but ended up tripping before he dropped the ball in front of the line. It took forever to get to the pins. He didn't care. Patient kid, he just laid there on his stomach like a slug, his chin resting on his hands, and watched until it got to the end.

Dad sat down in between turns but jumped up every few minutes to demonstrate a technique or fix something we were doing wrong. I bowled a seven on my turn. I thought sevens were okay but Dad said I had a hook. My arm twisted funny when I let go of the ball and it rolled all the way over to the right. He kept hopping up to hold my arm straight and show me.

"I've got it. I can go straight now." I let go and watched the ball roll into the gutter, saved only by the bumpers which knocked it back into the lane.

Dad sighed and said, "What a hook..." shaking his head. He tried to help. But I didn't think he got it. I really didn't care what the score was. At least that's what I told him. We talked in between turns.

"So how's school, Cassie?"

"Good. We have a lot of projects this month—all related to family."

He nodded.

"We'll be doing a family tree, and tracing our history and then doing some special projects that we get to create on our own."

"That sounds interesting. Anything I can help with?" He looked mildly distracted watching Ben take his turn.

"Well I might need some ideas for my special project, but I'll let you know."

"Okay. It's your turn Cassie."

***

We bowled pretty good in the first game but not so good in the second. We only got 50s in the second game so Dad won again. He never let us win, not even once. We didn't mind though. Dad always said the winner had to pay for the sundaes. We grabbed hot dogs at the bowling alley—which we knew Dad wasn't crazy about—but it was easier to eat here and then get sundaes afterwards. Friendly's was the best sundae place around.

At Friendly's, everything was pink-and-white striped, and Dad said it looked like the old-fashioned soda fountains he went to when he was a kid. The waitress came over and wiped our table clean with a damp cloth. Her uniform looked like ice cream, with a light pink dress and a white scalloped apron. She pulled out her ordering pad and pencil and looked at Dad, waiting.

"Yes, I'll have a cup of coffee and a dish of vanilla ice cream please."

She scribbled on the pad. "And for the children?"

"Ben?" My father pressed him to order.

"Umm. Buttercrunch ice cream with butterscotch sauce on it."

"A sundae?" The waitress asked. She reminded me a little of Nana Peterson, except this lady wore her glasses on a little silver chain, instead of on top of her head like Nana did.

Ben nodded.

"Nuts and whipped cream?"

"Yep. And extra cherries."

She smiled. "Extra cherries..." she said with more scribbling on the pad. She turned to me. "And you, dear?"

I hadn't definitely decided yet. Did I want sherbet or mint? Gooey caramel or drippy fudge? Indecisive, I settled on an old favorite. "I'll have a banana split with one scoop orange sherbet and fudge sauce, one scoop peppermint stick and pineapple topping and the last scoop black raspberry with marshmallow on it."

"Okay, that sounds like a masterpiece."

I smiled. Sundaes were like paints to me and I was the artist. There were so many marvelous creations. Dad, however, didn't see it that way. He was frowning at me.

"What's the matter, Dad?"

"Cassidy, are you ever going to outgrow your need to experiment with your food? Really, such grotesque combinations—"

I considered this. "Probably not. And they're not grotesque—they're creative."

He sighed loudly.

"Besides, I can't help it if I like all kinds of ice cream. It's hard to pick just one. And—I could *never* order vanilla."

"Vanilla? Why not?"

"It's so plain. It's like telling the whole restaurant you have absolutely no imagination. Mrs. Frazier is always telling us to be individuals and not to be afraid to use our imaginations. She says many people lose theirs when they grow up and we have to be very careful not to let ours get rusty."

He groaned. "Hmm. So now I have no imagination. Well, I wasn't much for creativity anyway. There's too much to do and too little time in which to do it in."

I shrugged. His response had proved my point.

"Don't worry Dad," Ben piped up. "Sometimes I get vanilla," he offered cheerfully. "But then I always get caramel on it so it's nice and gooey."

Dad looked unconsoled. I changed the subject.

"Dad, what kind of food did you eat as a little kid?"

"All kinds—why?"

"Well, I need to know about some recipes from your heritage for our Family Month project. Mom gave me her grandmother's strudel recipe and I need some ideas from your family too."

"I don't know. We ate what every American family ate—meatloaf, spaghetti, scrambled eggs..."

"How about your grandparents, then? What did they eat?"

"Well, I suppose the same things, basically. My father was Irish and your grandmother is English. Dad was a plain old meat-and potatoes guy, but your grandma used to make scones and her special raspberry tea..."

"That's good! What other English stuff did she make?"

"She made her own chips sometimes."

"She made you potato chips from scratch?"

"No, the British call french fries 'chips'. She used to peel potatoes, which my Dad loved, but she'd make them into chunky strips and fry them. They looked more like fingers than french fries but they tasted great."

His eyes lit up when he said this. I had never seen Dad get excited over any food.

"Can you show me how to make them maybe?"

"I would think so. Why?"

"For my class. I want to do something really original for my Family Month project." Then the idea hit me. "I think I'll call it a Round the World dinner. For different kinds of food, I'll bring in something from each family member's heritage— like Mom's German strudel and your English fries—stuff like that. I bet it would be better to bring in the real thing instead of just a boring recipe—don't you think?"

"Absolutely," he smiled, taking a sip of his coffee. "That sounds like a terrific idea. It's a deal then. You tell me when you need it and we'll cook them up together."

"Awesome." I was psyched. This project was going to be a hit and Dad even liked my idea. We'd have some German apple strudel and some English fries and scones, and some kind of Irish meat... It was going to be fantastic! Hey—maybe Josh could contribute some of his fabulous pasta. I decided not to mention this part to Dad. Things were going well enough. A dinner from around-the-world. This would be amazing. I finished my ice cream and planned my awesome project ahead. The pieces were all coming together.

"We should do this more often," Dad said, finishing his coffee.

"Well, how come we don't?" I asked, trying really hard not to sound too pushy. "You can ask me and Ben to go out anytime, right Ben?" I nudged him in the arm. He was busy slurping butterscotch off his fingers.

"Sure Dad. We should go out all the time," Ben said still making goopy sounds with his thumb and teeth.

"Why have you canceled so much lately?" I asked, trying to keep the anger out of my voice.

He flagged the waitress down for the check. I don't think she saw him since she went the other way to wait on some customers that had just sat down.

Dad sighed loudly in the waitress' direction. He turned back to us. "Hasn't your mother told you? Work has been so hectic over the past few months. I have a couple of major accounts that are taking all my time," Dad explained.

"But don't you miss us? We're more important than work," Ben said with a pout.

"Of course I miss you guys. But it's not always that easy—"

The waitress came with the check and Ben asked for a "to go" cup and straw for his drink. Dad pulled out his wallet and handed the waitress a credit card. He turned back to Ben and me.

"You'll understand when you get a little older. Sometimes you have to do things you don't want to. Jobs can be tough sometimes. Things don't always work out the way you planned."

"Well, can you try harder to see us more often and make up for the past few months?"

I couldn't tell if he was getting impatient or if this was just his tired voice. "I'll try," he sighed. "But the two of you have to promise me something too, okay?"

"What?" Ben and I said in unison.

"Promise me if I can't make it on some weekends, you'll try to understand, okay?"

I considered this. I tried every weekend.

"Okay," said Ben as he slid out of the booth and grabbed his jacket.

"Cassie?" My father looked at me.

"I'll try," I promised.

"Thank you," he said as he patted me on the head. "I'm doing the best I can."

It's funny. That's what Mom says all the time too. Must be a grown-up thing. I'm doing my best too, but I never think to say it out loud to anyone. It's just something I know.

Chapter Nine
The Argument

"So what's the deal with next weekend?" Marcy asked as she plopped down beside me on the bed.

"I don't know what we're doing yet, but Dad said he was coming for me and Ben sometime Saturday morning. Hey, I don't care what we do. Bowling was a blast last weekend, and I think he's trying to make up for lost time lately by seeing us two weekends in a row."

"That's good," Marcy said. She reached to retrieve a picture from the top of my desk, positioned by the head of my bed. She ran her fingers over the frame of smooth, polished blue and grey stones. The picture captured a day at the beach, this past summer. The smiling faces of Mom, Ben, Josh, and me—all huddled together in bright shore sunshine. We squatted in front of a huge sand castle with home-made flags of toothpicks and aluminum foil, a popsicle stick bridge, and seashell doors. The moat was half-full of water and looked only seconds away from caving in. Marcy turned to show me the picture. "This looks like fun," she said, "building such a great castle."

"Yeah," I said. "It was an awesome day."

"That guy Josh?" Marcy gestured to the picture. "He seems really great."

"Yeah." I pulled out my pocketbook and began to sort through its contents. I found a brush and fluffed up my bangs. "He's a good friend and all. But I still think it'll be strange having him live here, at least at first."

"Really?"

I shrugged. "Well, it won't be terrible," I said, pausing. I emptied my pocketbook onto the bed. Without thinking, I collected gum wrappers, tissues, and receipts and tossed them into the white wicker waste basket under my desk. I separated the change into piles. The pennies would go into my old teddy bear bank. The good change—quarters especially—I'd keep in my change purse. "It just means he's really gone," I said to Marcy, without looking up.

"Who is?"

"Dad. He's officially out of the picture when Josh marries Mom."

"It must be hard," said Marcy. "But it probably won't be that different. Your Dad's lived away for awhile now. It just means you'll still see him but Josh will be living here."

I ignored her reasoning, knowing she was probably right. My semi-bad mood was taking over and I needed time to sulk. "It's not like Dad was the perfect father or anything. I'm not stupid. I can see that. But he is my real father."

"Yeah, but he's not dead, Cassie. He's still around. He's still your father. He just doesn't live with you."

"It's just not the same," I said with a sigh.

Marcy didn't say anything.

"You don't have any idea what it's like," I said. "You've got both parents. Together. In the same house. The same original parents you started out with." I picked up the family tree I'd been working on and held it up in front of Marcy. Little paper labels dangled off the real tree branch, each member occupying a tiny limb. "Not my family—" I said, snapping a twig from the tree. Dad's branch. "It's broken. I don't even get a whole tree."

"I don't know what to say, Cassie." She bent to pick up the twig from the floor.

"Leave it alone!" I snapped. "I don't care. This was a dumb assignment anyway. Don't you think this was a stupid homework assignment?" I glared at her.

"Oh w-well—" she stammered. "I thought it was kind of fun, you know? Better than the usual president and state capitals stuff."

"You would think this was fun. I'll talk to you later," I said as I stood up and left my room, leaving Marcy sitting on the bed.

I rushed downstairs and grabbed my coat from the railing. I left Marcy's jacket on the banister. Slipping on one sleeve, I flew past the kitchen, through the living room and out the front door.

Saturday. At least I didn't have to watch Ben today. Freedom. I needed peace. Marcy didn't have a clue anyway. I crossed the street and headed for the little patch of farmland up the road. The cornfield was a wonderful thinking place.

The late-autumn sky was a brilliant icy blue. Cold, clear sunshine made the dusting from the season's first snowfall sparkle. Even thought it was November, the world was white, frozen, except for the little trail of muddy puddles that lined the sidewalk. Trucks and cars rushed past, some careful not to drown me with puddle spray. I quickened my pace. The wind froze my cheeks, my fingers, my eyes.

Nobody understood. So what if Josh was nice? He wasn't real. He couldn't be on my family tree. He wasn't my father or anything. Dad wrecked everything. It was final. Permanent. He wasn't coming back. I knew the divorce already did this but Mom getting remarried seemed to change everything forever. I remembered what my friend Liz had said when Mom and Dad first separated. She knew about this because her parents had split up a bunch of times. "First, somebody moves out after a big fight," she had informed me. "But it's no big deal. They just get separated for awhile. Then, they usually get back together."

"Are you sure?" I remembered asking her back then, seeking assurance from her. "Always?"

"Well, no, not always," she had responded. "But most of the time. Hey—don't worry about it. It'll be fine."

But I had worried about it. Not all of the time, but off and on. What if Dad never came back? But then, what if he did? Would the fighting come back too? Couldn't they work it out? I reached the fenced-in yard where the Furbers' horses grazed. The graceful, taffy-colored horse was out, and a group of cows bent nibbling at a patch of grass in the corner of the yard. I stared into the faded yellow-green of winter grasses, dotted here and there with the black and white of the Furburs' cows. They wandered slowly from here to there, pausing to nibble or look up, their whole world simple, slow, easy. I leaned against the wooden post-rail fence, balancing one foot onto the lower beam. The wind was brisk and cooled my thoughts.

What if Josh did come to live with us? Would that be so bad? He was nice, a real friend, so good to Mom. But a secret part of me wanted desperately for things to be the way they used to be. A family wasn't a guest house like the one we had rented last summer. It was supposed to be stable, permanent, secure. Additions would be okay—a new baby, new friends or neighbors maybe—but the real family should be together forever.

I squinted out over the field into the sun until my eyes stung. In spite of the cold, the sun still burned bright, shining white-gold in the pale sky. I stayed until it began to set over the field, sweeping through the sky in a slow, smooth descent.

Pale peach and lavender colored the sky with November pastels, the sunset soft and soothing. The sky listened. It heard me, maybe even understood. But what was I going to do? Nothing. Say nothing, and do nothing. That was probably the best strategy. Maybe I could talk to Dad this weekend. I decided to wait and see. If the time was right, maybe I'd talk to him.

It was time to go. I pulled away from the fence and turned toward home. I thought about Marcy. She had such a perfect life sometimes. Deep down, I also knew things weren't a fairy tale at Marcy's. I just said all those mean things to Marcy to get back at her, to hurt. Maybe then Marcy would know what it was like to have somebody really hurt her. Calmer now, I quickened my pace in the cold. It was almost dinnertime. Maybe I should call Marcy and apologize. Marcy's Dad hardly spent any time with her. So what if he was the real thing?

I decided I would definitely call Marcy after supper. But what about the tree...what was I going to do about that project? A little glue? Start from scratch? I decided to fix it tonight. No need for anyone to know what happened. Marcy wouldn't tell. She was a good friend. Plus, I still had some time before it was due. Time to think...

I neared the entrance to my street and turned into the wind. The sun was almost set now and the dusk made everything feel more chilly, more lonely. I thought about home, the warmth, the light in the windows. Something screeched behind me.

I fell to the ground and felt the pavement smack my forehead with an awful *squish* sound as my face hit the icy road. My palms scraped and burned when I tried to break my fall.

Chapter Ten
In The Hospital

I awoke to a room of white, lit only by a small overhead fluorescent bulb over my bed, and whispers—the muffled, low tones of Mom and Josh talking. Where was I? What had happened? I tried to lift my head. It hurt. Something pounded. I reached to rub my forehead but instead of skin I felt the rough, scratchy surface of a bandage. I squinted toward the windows at Mom, who was turned slightly away from me.

"Mom?" I whispered.

Mom stood up and rushed over to me, followed by Josh. Her face had that worried look etched into her mouth and forehead.

"What's going on?" I asked her, feeling sore and tired at the same time. Josh looked worried too. He bent to touch my shoulder as Mom sat beside me on the bed.

"You're all right. Everything will be fine." She smoothed the hair around my bandaged forehead. "Honey, you had an accident. A car hit you on our street. Some woman on her way home from the supermarket. She said it was dark. She couldn't see you. She was hysterical. The police came and an ambulance brought you here. Mrs. Phillips down the street called us. We heard sirens but we didn't know what it was." Tears filled her eyes. She swallowed. "It was you, honey. You were hurt. But you're going to be just fine."

"I don't remember much. Just the cold and my head squishing against the ground."

"How do you feel, kid?" Josh asked me, his voice husky, almost a whisper.

"My head hurts. Tired."

"It's okay, you've had a rough day. You have a mild concussion, but you'll feel better real soon. You get some rest now." He leaned to kiss me on the forehead, and then rose and walked to the doorway. He motioned to Mom. "I'll be in the hall." He left us alone in the quiet dimness of the room.

Mom hugged me. "I'm so glad you're all right, honey. We didn't know what to do. All we could do was wait...and pray..."

"Where's Ben?"

"He's at home with the Crosbys next door. We had to hurry. We didn't know how you were." She hesitated. "What he would have seen—" her voice trailed off. "It doesn't matter now. You're all right. You'll be just fine in a few days. That's all that matters."

"Where's Dad?"

"Honey, I called him but there was no answer. I left a message that it was urgent, and I hope to hear from him by the time I get back home."

The nurse came in and encouraged me to get some rest "Visiting hours are over," she said softly. "A good night's sleep can really make a difference."

"Mom, can you call Marcy and tell her I'm here?" I asked quietly.

"Sure, honey," Mom said as she left the room.

This was all so unbelievable. I sighed and closed my eyes. It felt like such a long day, a weird day. Everything seemed so far away—Marcy, the fight, the broken tree. Dad not being home with us anymore. Josh was here to stay... Too much to think about. I drifted off to sleep, my head throbbing from either the accident or too much thinking.

***

Morning came cheerfully with the bright November sun streaming through the hospital windows. A worker in blue and white scrubs walked briskly into the room with a stack of pink papers—today's menus. She handed one to me, smiled, and said "Good morning." She pulled a pencil from the drawer beside my bed and placed it on the breakfast stand next to the night table.

I stretched and rubbed my eyes. "I'm hungry."

"Good thing," said the nurse. "There's a lot to choose from."

I scanned the menu—cereal, pancakes, eggs, juice, toast, coffee... Coffee! I hated coffee. Other than that, the rest sounded great. I checked off all of the above. Toast over English muffins, fruit cup over grapefruit. Skip the cottage cheese—diet food. Mom would have loved cottage cheese. Dad would have asked if they had Eggs Benedict.

Before long, Mom and Ben came by. Sunday. Ben was going to miss Sunday school. He looked pleased. Guess he owed me one. He rushed over to me and pounced on the bed. The bounce made my stomach churn.

"Ben, be careful!" Mom warned. "Cassie's head needs to heal."

Ben considered this and straightened his place on the bed, smoothing the covers. He smiled at me and held up a comic book, his reading for the day.

"So, are you okay?" He looked at me.

"Fine, Ben. Just a little tired. The whole thing was so strange."

He nodded, mimicking the way Josh did when he showed he understood a situation. But soon his attention shifted to the wall. His gaze fixed on the generously-sized television set mounted high on the wall opposite my bed.

"Cool!" He leaped off my bed. I watched him scan the room for the remote. Spying the clicker on the night table, he reached to play with the buttons. He flipped through the stations. "You can watch TV all day?" he asked me over his shoulder.

"Well, when I'm awake..."

"Wow! Mom I wanna stay here with Cass today," he announced, perching himself on the vinyl-covered armchair that sat by the windows.

I laughed and Mom shook her head. "We'll see, Ben," she said. She turned to me. "I want you to rest today. How are you feeling?"

"Much better now. I slept well."

"Well that's nice to hear. You needed it."

Mom retrieved some magazines from her bag. "I brought you these to read in case you get bored." She handed me a Teen and a Discovery Girls magazine. The covers had headlines about holiday dates and Christmas dresses.

"Ben?" Mom tried to get his attention. His eyes were fixed on a religious show. A tall, white-haired man was speaking about being saved. "Ben?" she called again, a little louder this time.

He barely looked up. "What?"

"Didn't you have something you wanted to give your sister?"

"What? Oh—" he said. "I almost forgot. Here," he said, pulling Patches, my worn but much-loved stuffed pig, from his jacket and tossing it to me. He turned back to the television.

Mom glared at him. "Your little brother was *so thoughtful*," she explained loudly. "He thought you might miss your pig. He suggested we bring him in so you don't get lonely."

I smiled. "Thanks, Ben" I called over to the chair in the corner. Patches wasn't like a baby doll or a little kid toy. He was a grown-up sort of pig. He even had a ribbon around his neck where I had pinned the buttons I collected. Some had funny sayings like "If wearer is found depressed, give chocolate immediately" or simple reminders like "Smile!". I had even pinned on the "Tin Grins Are In" one Marcy had gotten from the orthodontist.

"Hey Mom!" I straightened up. "Any news from Dad?"

"Not yet. I think he might be out of town. I'm sure he'll call as soon as he gets my message, honey."

"Can I call out on this phone?"

"You sure can," she said, "but your Dad isn't home."

"I know. I just wanted to see if maybe Marcy was home. We had a fight yesterday and I left really mad."

Mom flashed me a knowing look. She didn't ask what the fight was about. "Well, why don't you try and see if you can talk to her? We'll be going to run a few errands and we'll be back this afternoon. The doctor will be checking you today and pretty soon we'll find out when you're coming home."

"Great," I said, relaxing. I looked over at Ben and back to Mom. "You might have some trouble taking him with you."

"Ben. Ben. Come on, it's time to go..."

"Aw, Mom..."

"Now." He pulled himself from the chair and shuffled toward the door, his eyes still glued to the TV.

"Goodbye, honey" Mom said as she bent to kiss me on the cheek. "We'll be back in a little while." Ben lingered in the doorway. "Goodbye, Cassie," Mom reminded him.

"Bye Cass. See you later," he mumbled.

Chapter Eleven
Marcy To The Rescue

The next day things were pretty quiet and I decided to call Marcy. It wasn't her fault everything was such a mess. Just as I picked up the phone, I spotted her face in the doorway. Wearing jeans and a pink sweatshirt, she peered into the doorway as if she wasn't really sure what room I was in.

"Hey, Marcy," I called from my bed, surprised.

"Hi Cass—" she said slowly, as if I'd yell at her. "How are you feeling?" she said, finding a place beside my bed and seating herself with her back to the window.

"Not too bad," I answered, "but let me just say something first. I'm really sorry about the things I said when I walked out and left you in my room."

"Forget it. I do that too sometimes. It's okay to blame somebody—everybody has to let off some steam. Hey, that's what friends are for."

"Well, thanks for understanding."

She adjusted her place on the seat and twirled a strand of hair around her finger. "I was worried—"

"Me too. I guess anything like this makes you realize it could have been really serious. But the doctor said I'll be fine and I can go home soon."

"That's great," she said. "You were lucky."

"I know." Not wanting to think about what could have happened, I straightened up and reached for my pocketbook which Mom had slid into the top drawer of my night table. I grabbed my brush and a little pink lip gloss. I felt better already.

Marcy did the same. We were always giving each other make-overs. "You know, Cassie, I've been thinking too. It's okay to feel bad about your parents coming apart. I mean, I don't know what I'd do if my parents split up. I think you're really brave for handling everything so cool. You gotta have some days you flip out. Who wouldn't?"

"Thanks, Marcy."

She returned her lip gloss to her pocketbook. "Hey—I'll help you with your tree project if you want," she offered.

"No, don't worry about it. I'll just glue it or something. Mrs. Frazier won't care. If it ends up late, I can just say somebody fell out of my family tree and had to be glued back on."

Marcy laughed. "Whatever you say."

"Hey—I got some news," she changed the subject. "We got a cat from my neighbor down the street. She's moving to an apartment that won't allow pets and she asked if we'd take care of her kitty. Her name is Rosey and she'll be a friend for Pisces."

"I still can't believe you named your cat Pisces. It means fish," I insisted, shaking my head.

"But he was born in March. That makes him a Pisces."

"Does he know that? He'll probably need therapy."

"No he won't. He's a very well-adjusted cat. I already explained it to him. He thinks it's a cool name. Better than all his cat friends on our block."

I laughed and turned to reach my water glass on the night table. Pretty soon room service would serve my lunch. I spied the clock on the table. It said 11:30. Lunch would be here any minute. But wait— this was the middle of the day and it was Monday—so what was Marcy doing here?

"Hey—what's the deal with school?" I asked, surprised and embarrassed that I was still stuck thinking it was the weekend.

Marcy laughed. "I was wondering if you knew what day it was!" She shrugged. "I sort of skipped."

"Sort of? How do you sort of skip?"

"Easy. You see, school's there and I'm not, so technically I skipped. But Mom knows so it's not a parent secret or anything. In fact, she dropped me off."

"You skipped school and your mother drove you?"

She beamed at me. "Well, you're kind of a good reason, don't you think? It's not like I faked sick or anything."

I laughed. "Only at your house, Marcy." I watched as she pulled a bright purple balloon from her pocketbook and handed it to me. I looked at it. Small and deflated, it had little black lines all over it.

"A letter," said Marcy. "I wrote you a balloon letter. You have to blow it up to read it."

"Wow!" I said, impressed. Marcy was so creative. At summer camp, it was toilet paper. She had written a whole hidden words puzzle on it and we took turns circling the names of the cutest boys she had buried in between the rest of the alphabet. So now it was a balloon.

I stretched it and puffed it into shape. Blowing it up made me a little dizzy so Marcy had to help. I tried to wipe any spit off the balloon before I gave it to her but she just said it was no big deal. She handed it back to me to tie.

Marcy smiled at me and shrugged. "You know I stink at tying these things, and I always wreck my nail polish."

I looped the end around my finger and nearly cut off the circulation trying to make a knot. This was cool! My first Get-Well balloon. She had drawn a big smiley face on it and written all kinds of funny "It could be worse..." sayings. I turned it around and around to read all of the words. "It could be worse..." I read aloud "you could have been run over...

twice." "It could be worse... Brad MacPherson could have seen the whole thing—and thought you were a geek." "It could be worse...it could've been me!"

"This is awesome!" I exclaimed. Marcy beamed. She was always thinking up new ways for us to write letters or do fun things.

Before long, an orderly carried in lunch on a huge tray. I was so hungry I had forgotten what I had checked off this morning. There was a tuna sandwich, soup, a big shiny apple and a glass of milk. Plus there were crackers and a cup of steaming hot cocoa. The orderly winked at us. He was a tall thin guy who looked like he was in high school or early college.

Marcy smiled at him. He looked at the two of us and grinned back. "You here for the day?" he asked her.

She shrugged. "Yep. I'm here with my friend. All afternoon. Until she throws me out."

He laughed. "Tell you what. How about I sneak you in something for lunch?"

Before she could answer, he had whisked out of the room and returned a few minutes later with another tuna sandwich and a cup of cocoa. "Best I could do," he said as he placed the dish in front of Marcy.

"Thanks! Thanks a lot! I'm starving!"

We finished lunch in a hurry and Marcy took out some nail polish so we could do manicures. She said just cause I was in the hospital didn't mean I had to look grungy. By the afternoon we each had coral frost nail polish and she had freshly French-braided hair. I just got a ponytail since the bandages were in the way. I was tired but didn't want to waste this time sleeping. This was like a sleep-over. Best Monday home from school I ever had.

Marcy's mom came to pick her up a few minutes before my mother came back to spend supper with me. She left Ben at the neighbor's house and came by herself this time. She said Josh might come by later to say good night.

"How is everything, honey?" Mom asked me as she came into the room. "I left work a little early so I could come see you. Did you have fun with Marcy?"

I nodded, surprised she knew Marcy had come by.

My face must have asked the question because she added, "I saw her on the way out."

"Mom?"

"What is it?"

"Have you talked to Dad yet?"

"Well I called him again to tell him everything and let him know where you were. He has to be out of town."

I shook my head. Where was he? I didn't know what to make of this. Just then a nurse came into my room with a bright bunch of flowers.

"For you," she said cheerfully as she placed them on the windowsill. The sky was now dark and the lights of nearby buildings looked like little yellow squares against the purple-blue darkness of the sky.

"Who are they from?" I asked, as she turned to leave the room.

"Well, a florist just delivered them. There's a card."

Mom reached for the card and handed it to me. I opened the flap and slid it out of the tiny envelope. The card had the words "Get Well" on it, with a picture of a little duck holding a flower. On the inside I read, "Sorry I couldn't see you, honey. I just got your Mom's message and I'm coming home. Hope you're feeling better! Love, Dad."

116

While the flowers were nice, I was mad he hadn't come to see me. Work again. It was always some project or road trip. If I had really been hurt, I bet he'd have felt bad then.

Chapter Twelve
Eye Of The Hurricane

Morning came and the nurse woke me up by announcing

that the doctor would be in to see me shortly after breakfast. If

everything looked okay, I could be checked out of the hospital

by this afternoon.

"Great!" I said to the nurse as she crossed my room and

drew the curtains wide. It looked awesome outside—probably

freezing, but so bright and sunny it made all the frost on the

windows glittery. "Will the doctor have to take any more

blood?" I hoped not. The thought made my stomach tingle,

and I needed some assurance here. I hated not knowing until the doctor came in. They never told you anything. But the nurse looked helpful enough.

"I don't think so." She paused. "He'll probably do one last x-ray and talk to you for a few minutes. No more blood tests, I don't think." She said this kindly but as if it made no difference if they had to take blood or not. I guess I didn't look as afraid as I had thought when I asked the question.

I surveyed the room. With Patches propped up on my night table, the cards spread out on the windowsill, and my purple balloon letter from Marcy, the place looked pretty cheerful. For a little while, I had even forgotten about Dad, but the big flowery cards reminded me of that little card with the duck on it. A couple of tiny words said everything—and nothing. Dad was a whole new problem now. He never even came to see me. I wanted desperately to have some major reason, something incredible, to be the answer.

I imagined a big, ugly guy with spiked-up hair and scars all over his face hijacking Dad's plane as he hurried to fly home. Dad had risked his life for me and, shaken though he was, still managed to call a florist and have flowers delivered to his sick daughter. Poor Dad. And all he wanted was to come see me in the hospital.

"Good morning, honey. How did you sleep?" Mom brought me out of my daydream. She came with a plastic shopping bag in one arm.

"Clean clothes," she explained. "How are you feeling?"

"Fine," I said. "The doctor's coming in to see if I can go home today."

"That's wonderful!" Mom smiled at me.

The phone rang. It was close to the bed on the little night table, so I grabbed it before the second ring.

"Hello?"

"Hello, Cassidy? It's Dad."

"Dad?"

"Cassidy, I wanted to talk to you, about yesterday. I—"

"Were you hijacked?" I wanted to know.

He laughed. "Hijacked? No, I wasn't hijacked."

My heart sank.

"I had to fly to Dallas and I never checked my messages until yesterday. The nurse said I couldn't call late last night so I had to wait until this morning. I flew back as soon as I could.

I was afraid you'd think I wasn't there for you. I'll be in this very afternoon."

"You didn't come to see me because of some stupid work thing?"

"Cassidy, now try to understand. It's not stupid honey, it's what adults have to do sometimes. I'll come as soon as I can. I'm sorry."

"Not Mom. She has a job but she got here—*every* day. And Josh, he came too." I added that last part to sting him back. I hoped it worked. Mom came over and sat on my bed. My eyes started to blur and I blinked hard.

"Cassidy, I don't know what else to say. Did you like the flowers?"

The flowers! I pictured the bouquet in the bathroom where Mom had brought them to add water. I wish Mom had put them in the trash. Who needed his dumb flowers anyway?

I didn't know what else to say to him. I handed the phone to Mom and slid off of the bed. I grabbed some things for the shower and headed for the bathroom. Mom's voice trailed behind me. She spoke quickly into the receiver.

"Bill, she's upset. She needed to see you. It doesn't matter what the reason was. I think she's also going through a tough time with my remarriage. Why don't you try to call her again once we get home?"

I shut the door behind me, put my towels and stuff on the sink counter and undressed in a hurry. The air was still a little cold since it was early yet. I stepped into the shower and flipped on the faucet. The steamy water felt good. It washed away all the crummy feelings and made my skin and eyes and shoulders relax. I wished I could stay here. Who wanted to go home now? I had TV and magazines and Mom and Ben to visit and even Josh to stop by. Plus, the food wasn't so bad and the last couple days there were hardly any tests. Even Marcy got to come in and visit. Everything I could ever want.

I twirled and twirled in the shower and made my face go in and out of the spray like a tall sprinkler. Like a hurricane or a small tornado. I thought of Ben's storm talk about school. Maybe this was the eye of my hurricane, the quiet time, Dad's away time. Maybe I was the eye of the storm, the nothing place. Who needed Dad anyway? He probably wouldn't have stayed long —even if he did come in. I should have told him off. Maybe said I didn't care anyway because all the people that mattered had already shown up. Or I could have insulted his job and told him his company was boring and if he had to spend so much time at his job then maybe he wasn't very good at his career either. I could have kicked myself for not thinking of anything really good to say on the phone. That always happened. The perfect come-back never clicks into my head until days later. I lathered up a huge foam and stayed in the shower for a long time. At least half an hour. I looked like a raisin with my fingers all wrinkled from the water. So what? At least I was going to be really clean for the doctor.

By the time I got out of the shower, Mom was off the phone and she was packing up my clothes and stuff just in case the doctor said I could go home today. Mom looked at me when I put my dirty clothes into the plastic bag in the suitcase.

She gave me a hug. "Do you want to talk?"

"No, I'm okay. Dad's a jerk. His job is dumb. Aren't I more important than his *job*?"

"Than *any* job, honey. But he did fly back as soon as he could. He's trying Cassie. I know you're upset now, but remember that, if you can."

124

I said I'd try.

We didn't talk about it anymore. I didn't have anything else to say and I felt like Dad wasn't worth talking about if he didn't care about me. Maybe I'd talk to Marcy, though. Or maybe not. She still had a father and maybe she wouldn't understand. Then again, the balloon was just what I needed.

The doctor came in for a few minutes, talked to me, looked over his chart, and asked me how I was feeling. That was it! No blood tests. No more x-rays. He said I could go home and was ready to return to school. I felt like telling him now my stomach felt sick. My outsides may have been fine, but my insides were a mess.

Chapter Thirteen
Love Notes

"Shhhh!" Miss Storrigan spat in a very loud whisper. "This is a study hall, not recess." She eyed us over her wire-framed glasses. "If any of you don't have something to do, just come and see me and I'll give you enough to keep you busy."

Louie Carroll groaned but Miss Storrigan couldn't tell who made the noise so she didn't say anything more.

"See?" Marcy whispered as she pushed the foil toward me. "You have to wrap it really tight around the cardboard and then tape it on the back at the corners."

I looked at the square when she was done. The foil was really tight and shiny on the good side.

"Now you take a pencil—a dull one actually works best, so you don't scratch up the foil and tear the page—and you write whatever you want."

Another of Marcy's inventions—she was showing me how to make a letter out of aluminum foil. She said it was like engraving only easier and cheaper. Plus this was cool for a letter—something different instead of our usual crumpled up notebook paper.

I watched her carefully press the pencil into the foil. "And it shows up so you can read it?" I asked her.

"Yeah, see?" She scribbled 'I love Brad MacPherson' in a big heart with an arrow on the foil.

I stared at her, accusingly.

"For you!" she insisted. "I don't like him. Keith's more my type. But I think Brad likes you..."

"No, he doesn't. He hardly ever talks to me."

"He does too. At least he smiles at you sometimes and he sat next to you at lunch the other day."

"That's because there were no other seats left at his table!"

128

"Still, it's a good sign. A very positive sign."

Marcy could be such an optimist. No way did Brad know I liked him and he definitely didn't like me. I was very sure of that. I looked over at him sitting by the windows in the back of the room. He was playing with his pencil in one hand and held a book in the other. Brad didn't seem to like anybody in particular. He was just cute and the girls knew it, but he didn't show what he was thinking. Some of the girls thought he was a flirt, but he never really did anything flirty. It was just that smile. He just seemed like such a nice guy and that smile was so cute that a lot of girls really liked him. But nobody could tell with Brad MacPherson. So far, no one knew if he ever liked somebody back. And as far as I was concerned, Brad hardly knew me, so I doubted I was anything special. Plus I hardly ever talked to him, so why would he like me?

I drew a little heart next to Marcy's big heart on the foil before Louie Carroll walked by and snatched the letter off my desk.

"No!" I yelled, forgetting the quiet rules of study.

"Cassidy Phillips, is there a problem?"

I shook my head. "No... Well, see I had a... Louie took my..."

"Louie took your what, Miss Phillips?"

"Nothing. I don't have a problem, Miss Storrigan."

"I beg to differ, Miss Phillips," Louie interrupted. He held my aluminum foil letter up for the whole class to see.

"Miss Storrigan, we do have a problem here," he announced as he walked to the front of the room.

Miss Storrigan looked as if her patience was running out. "Louie," she warned. "Take your seat. You are interrupting the class for everybody in the room."

But he just walked over to the teacher's desk and smiled. All eyes were on him and even Miss Storrigan looked surprised. Kids didn't test her that often but Louie broke all the rules. He wasn't afraid of anybody. He could spend half his life in detention and nobody would notice.

He spoke loud enough for everyone to hear. "We have a problem here, Miss Storrigan."

"Louie, what is going on?"

He pointed to my letter and read out loud. "I love Brad MacPherson. That's the kind of filth Cassidy Phillips is writing in study hall."

Oh my God. He read it out loud to everyone. "I didn't write that, Miss Storrigan."

The class all yelled "Ooh—Cassie loves Brad—" in unison and a bunch of kids were laughing.

I felt dizzy. I couldn't even turn to look at Brad but I bet he was laughing too. Suddenly the whole room felt hot and my neck was all sweaty. Everybody was staring at me. God, just take me out of here. Make this be a dream. Make there be a fire drill so I can leave and change schools.

"Cassidy," Miss Storrigan called over the laughter in the room. "Who wrote this?"

"Umm, we were just..."

She stared at me and I couldn't even explain. All the words were mixed up in my head but nothing came out of my mouth. I looked at Marcy but she was already talking.

"It's just a note. We were practicing with foil and—" She flashed me a helpless look and shrugged.

I wanted to cry. I wanted to crawl under my desk. I wanted to kill Louie Carroll.

"Never mind, girls. That's enough. Do you have homework to do? Let's do something a bit more productive. I'm sure you can find something else to keep you busy. If you can't, I'll be glad to give you an assignment for the rest of the period."

"Umm, no. We're all set," Marcy explained for the both of us.

But I just wanted to die. Either that or get a pass to the girls' room and never come out.

Chapter Fourteen
Test Tube Revenge

I felt sick all morning as I got dressed and thought about study hall yesterday. I changed clothes three times. I tossed my sweater dress on the bed—nothing dressy—or Brad would definitely think I was desperate. The gray sweats came off too since anything too slouchy would make the kids think I looked too ugly to even think about liking such a cute guy. I settled finally on jeans and a navy sweater, not because I was happy as much as Mom kept calling up the stairs for me to hurry or I'd miss the bus. Trying for the invisible look, I checked my reflection in the mirror one last time and prayed silently that nobody would notice me today. Perhaps even better, no one would care.

Homeroom seemed pretty normal and Marcy was great. She promised me last night she'd do her best to stick with me today so I wouldn't cry or do something embarrassing if anyone made a crack about Brad. My stomach knotted as the bell rang and it was time for science class. Mr. Jenkins had no sense of humor and I couldn't stand it if he heard what happened the other day and said anything in class.

Today started the third week of our biology unit, and Mr. Jenkins had lined all of our lab tables with white doctor's office paper and racks of test tubes. We were to work in teams, and thankfully, Marcy was my partner. The miracle I prayed for didn't happen, as Brad MacPherson showed up for school and was seated quietly behind me at the next table. Some kids in his group laughed. My face reddened. What was so funny? I strained to listen when Marcy nudged me to help with the fermentation experiment. I stared at the layers of yellow and clear liquid in the tube with complete disinterest. Who cared about silly test tubes and experiments when life itself was falling apart?

Before I could turn around, someone had pasted something to my back. I saw that it was Louie Carroll and he had this big, obnoxious smirk on his face. I couldn't even look Brad's way. Louie wasn't in his group but I was sure everyone saw. And that meant Brad too. Marcy revealed the "something" as masking tape and saw that the tape was attached to a piece of notebook paper. She crumpled it behind her back and tried to shove it in her pocket without showing it to me.

"What does it say?" I pushed, my face feeling hot and sweaty.

"Nothing. It's stupid. You don't want to know."

"Marcy, let me see it. I can't take this garbage from idiot Louie and just pretend he didn't do anything. Give it to me."

She pulled it from her pocket and handed to me. A bunch of kids were snickering as I opened the letter and saw a huge lipstick drawn mouth in the shape of a kiss. The note said "This one's for you, Brad" in magic marker. Tears stung my eyes as I tore up the note and shoved the little pieces of paper under the table.

I was so mad I couldn't think straight. Marcy ducked under the table and grabbed all the little pieces before Mr. Jenkins could see. He hated notes and I sure didn't want another "Brad" note read aloud in class. He passed up the aisle between the tables and was three steps away when Marcy saw one last scrap of paper and shoved it into the test tube. What was she thinking? Now he'd know for sure! A little square of paper floated in the yellow liquid inside the tube. She swished it around and tried to fish it out but it was too late.

"How are we doing here, ladies?" Mr. Jenkins eyed our experiment without picking up the tube. "Any questions about the layering here? Remember, we are watching the excess alcohol float to the top and evaporate into the air. If we check these tubes tomorrow the fluid will be half the level it is right now."

We nodded, not looking up.

It was then that Louie approached the table and picked up the tube. "Mr. Jenkins, their experiment here doesn't look like everyone else's. How come they have a little white thing in the tube that we don't?"

Mr. Jenkins looked surprised at Louie's sudden interest in biology and he bent to inspect the tube itself. "Mr. Carroll, you are right. This is a different effect going on here." He looked at us. "Ms. Nickerson, Ms. Phillips, any idea what has happened here? Did you follow the directions and rinse the tubes first?"

I nodded while Marcy said, "Oh, no, Mr. Jenkins. We thought you meant to rinse the tube afterward. You know, cleaning up all this stuff after we're done." She straightened, looking more certain of herself. "That's what it must be. I bet the tube wasn't perfectly clean."

Looking slightly annoyed with us for not following directions, Mr. Jenkins just shook his head and said "all right then, but next time read everything before you start. It could get you into trouble if you don't."

Not satisfied with the teacher's response, Louie reached into the tube to fish out the piece of paper. It was frayed and soggy in the tube but you could still see a little lipstick on it. He stuck his finger into the glass and pressed further into the

137

tube until the paper was almost within reach. Marcy shoved him behind Mr. Jenkins back and told him to leave us alone.

"Knock it off, Louie. You are such a jerk."

"Oh, protecting your little lovesick friend. How sweet," he crooned.

"Shut up," I said. I couldn't think of anything else to say. Nothing clever or cutting came to mind, just the same old remark I had used since second grade when a kid had told me my hair ribbons made me look like a baby.

"Oh, shut up," Louie mimicked back to me, his finger now wedged all the way into the test tube.

Mr. Jenkins turned around and spotted him leaning on the table with the tube on his finger. "Mr. Carroll, what are you doing?"

"I was trying to find out what that little white thing was."

"That's enough. Leave the ladies alone and take your seat."

In an unusual act of obedience, he stood up and walked back to his lab table, with our test tube still attached.

"Mr. Carroll?"

Louie looked up.

"Leave the test tube behind. It belongs on Ms. Nickerson and Ms. Phillips table. You have your own tube."

He shrugged and walked back to the table, shaking the tube as he went. He pulled with his left hand. It didn't move. He shook his right hand really hard until all the liquid got bubbly, but it still didn't budge off his finger. It was stuck. Louie got the test tube stuck onto his finger and he couldn't get it off!

"Is there a problem, Mr. Carroll?"

"Umm, yes sir there is," said Louie only a little bit sarcastically. "You see, well, I was trying to help these young ladies out with their experiment and I guess this tube is a little smaller than I thought..."

Keith started laughing and I saw that Brad was laughing too. Mr. Jenkins frowned. He turned to Marcy and me. "He was helping you?"

"No he was not," said Marcy loudly. "He was being a pain and we told him to knock it off and leave us alone."

"He wouldn't go away," I added meekly, still embarrassed about the love note taped to my back that started this whole mess.

Mr. Jenkins nodded, knowingly. "This isn't the first time you've done something irresponsible Louie so I cannot say I am surprised. Aren't we a little more mature than a curious toddler?"

For probably the first time in his life, Louie said nothing.

Mr. Jenkins frowned again. "Mr. Carroll, you will receive a pass to the nurse's office to see about that test tube. Then you will receive two days' detention for disrupting our class and behaving irresponsibly. Is that clear? I will send a letter home to your parents if you do not attend detention. See you tomorrow afternoon."

Louie stood up and got the pass from Mr. Jenkins. The teacher sent Mark Peterson, the class aide, to go with Louie to make sure he got all the way to the nurse's office without making some detour into trouble. As Louie approached the door, Mr. Jenkins spoke again.

"Mr. Carroll? One more thing. You owe this class an apology."

Louie stared at him.

"Now."

"For what?" Louie faked an expression of disbelief.

"For disrupting our entire class and interfering with the education of students who want to learn."

"Yeah, right."

Boy did he have guts. Or sand for brains as Dad sometimes said.

"What was that Mr. Carroll?" But without letting him repeat it, he pointed to Louie's finger and said, "Do you want to remain in this room with that test tube as your companion for the rest of your days here at Piedmont?

Louie grimaced at his finger, now white and swollen inside the tube. "Sorry," he muttered before plowing through the door with Mark Peterson at his heels.

***

Class ended soon after that and I rushed to get out of the room without another word to anyone. I couldn't tell what everybody else thought but I was psyched Louie got what he deserved—or at least a little taste of what he deserved.

But what did Brad think? He wasn't really good friends with Louie but he wasn't an enemy either. Did he think I was such a slug to deserve that note? Was it funny to him?

Wondering about it made me sick to my stomach. I thought Marcy could tell because I felt a tap on my shoulder as I made it to the door. But it wasn't Marcy. It was Brad.

I pretended not to see him and turned back around to leave when I felt a tap again.

"Cassidy."

This time I couldn't ignore him. He said my name. That gorgeous velvety voice had said my name.

I tried to look indifferent. "What?"

He whispered so no one else could hear. "I didn't do it."

"What?"

"I didn't tell Louie to write that note."

"You didn't?"

"No. It was mean. I'm sorry." He smiled and shrugged. "Hey, you got back at him in the long run, huh?"

I laughed, tentatively. "Yeah, I guess I did, huh?"

"Forget it," he said and patted me on the shoulder, before stepping out of the room and disappearing down the hall.

Chapter Fifteen
The Phone Call

Mom and Josh stood in the kitchen, surrounded by bowls and pans and spoons. On the stove, the counter, the table, everywhere—there were utensils and containers full of ingredients and warm dinner smells. It was Italian night, as Mom called it— spaghetti night as Josh and Ben and I had come to call it. Once a week now, for several months, Josh and Mom got together to cook a fabulous supper of pastas and sauces and salads. But the cooking was the fun since Josh was an experimenter. He made Ben and me try to guess what was in the sauce each week and the one who got closest got to choose the dessert for the next week.

"No, Cassidy, I want you and Ben to be on equal footing for this one," he said, pulling me away from the counter so I couldn't sneak a peek.

"Aw, come on..." I protested. This was part of the game. The challenge to guess Josh's next creation. I swear the guessing was almost as fun as the eating.

"Fine, then," he feigned a sophisticated voice. "If you won't leave, then I'll cover..." He grabbed a large towel from a nearby drawer and draped it over the counter so I couldn't inspect the collection of spices and jars and bottles that would comprise his next concoction.

Mom had abandoned us in the kitchen to go retrieve Ben from his room.

"So what's new with school, Cass? Any boyfriends I should meet?"

How in the world did he know? Was he psychic?

I shrugged. I couldn't lie to Josh. There was something so nice about him, so open. Like he wouldn't flip out no matter what I said.

"Well, as a matter of fact. There's a boy I kind of like, but Marcy wrote this stupid thing to practice making a foil letter and now everyone thinks I like him."

"But you just said you do like him."

"I do, but I didn't want anyone to *know* I like him."

"Oh," he nodded, with a knowing look. "I remember those days. Not too long ago, as I recall." He turned his back and grabbed an anonymous jar to sprinkle into the pot on the stove. "Those were the days when the knowing was worse than the liking. It wasn't cool to be anything but a very *secret* admirer."

I nodded. "You got it. It's the same way now." I looked up at him. He was so cool. "I guess some things don't change then, huh?"

He shook his head, smiling at me. "No, I guess they never do."

***

I got up before everybody else and the house was still quiet. It was Saturday and cloudy, but a little early to tell what the weather would be like today. I started the woodstove in the living room with a few kindling sticks from the bucket and tore newspaper into strips to get the little match flame going. I loved fires, especially on gloomy days, and it made the winter not seem so cold and dark.

Two weeks had gone by since Mrs. Frazier introduced Family Month and I had a lot of work to do on my dinner project. Then there was the Family Tree—no places for anybody that really fit. Somebody always lost room or the tree just didn't represent my whole family.

The phone rang. Startled, I jumped up to answer it before anyone else woke up. The kitchen clock said 7:30 and I was surprised someone would call so early.

"Hello?"

"Cassidy? It's Dad."

"Oh, it's you." I had made myself unavailable two times earlier when he tried to call me after I got home from the hospital, but I felt trapped this time. I took a deep breath. "Hi, Dad."

"I wanted to know if we could talk. I wanted to apologize to you for not making it back in time to visit you in the hospital."

I said nothing.

"I know that hurt your feelings, but Cassie, please trust me honey. I did everything I could. I didn't want to be away when you needed me."

He sounded sad. This made me understand a little. Maybe it wasn't his fault. Maybe it was me—everything was a problem, everything a hurt.

"It's okay, Dad," I said. "I just miss you."

"I miss you too, honey."

"Will you still help with the English fries?"

"I'll be there!" His tone brightened, and I felt better now. "Cass?"

"Yeah?"

"I love you. I always love you."

"I love you too, Dad," I said back, my eyes tearing. We hadn't said that in a long time.

Chapter Sixteen
Kitchen Concoction

"Apricots! You put preserves into the sauce?"

Josh nodded. "And what else? Come on—guess at least one thing."

"Oregano."

He shook his head. "No way—that's a totally different taste. Oregano and parmesan are all traditional flavors for sauce. This one's more sweet-and-sour."

We stood in the middle of the kitchen, loading the dishwasher. Dinner was over and Mom had left us to clean up in here while Ben finished his homework in the living room and she rushed to finish some chores upstairs.

"Pineapple."

"Great! You're right. Now you're thinking sweet-and-sour."

"I don't know what else but I guessed pineapple and Ben gave up guessing. So can I still pick dessert for next week?"

He smiled. "Sure."

"Pudding. Banana pudding with mandarin oranges in it."

"Cool Whip on top!" hollered Ben from the next room.

"Oh, all right," I mockingly gave in. "But no cherries."

"No way!" he protested. "You can't have whipped cream without cherries." After a pause, he said "Fine, then I'll just put cherries on mine and the rest of you people don't get to have any. I'll eat all the wonderful cherries myself."

Josh and I laughed. Even Mom was smiling at our game as she returned from putting the laundry away.

"Hey, Mom?"

"What?" she called from the living room over the noise of the television.

"I need you to show me how to make the strudel that Nana makes. You promised and I have to bring it in this Friday for class."

"Oh, it's that soon?" She paused and added, "Well then we'll have to make a shopping list to make sure we don't forget anything. How many people are in your class?"

Mom was so organized. "We have 27 kids plus Mrs. Frazier."

"Okay, we'll keep that in mind and triple Nana's recipe."

"Sounds good to me."

I turned to Josh. "Say, Josh—do you want to add to my Round-the-World dinner?"

"Sure," he shrugged. "Sounds interesting. What is it?"

"For class it's Family Month and we're doing projects that show different things about our families. It can be anything but cooking is one idea and it's not the only project I'm doing but I'll tell you this one first. You can bring in a recipe for a food that shows your family's background—like German or English or Italian—and then make the food and bring it in to class so everyone can try it."

"Oh, and you said you're making your Nana's strudel."

"I am. But Mom doesn't even know this part because I haven't decided exactly what else I'm making..."

He looked confused so I tried to explain. "I wanted to include Dad's family too and not leave anyone out. So he's going to show me how to make British chips— those are *french fries*—" I explained, "and maybe I'll get a recipe for Grandma's scones too."

"Wow! You'll sure be doing a lot of cooking for this class. Do you want to make peanut butter ice cream too? That's one of your specialties now!"

I laughed. "No. That's not an ethnic food that shows something about our history. But..."

"What?" he said suspiciously. "You want me to make something else for you?"

"No, you can't make it. It's my project so I have to cook. But I can have help with something else you've shown me." Without waiting for his guess I said, "One of your pastas!"

He looked pleased. "But I have two questions."

"What?"

"First, this is supposed to be Family Month. Are you sure you want one of my recipes?"

I knew what he was getting at. "It doesn't matter. You're already like family and you'll be a real part of my family in a few months. You're marrying Mom aren't you?"

He laughed. "I guess I'm marrying all of you."

He really was too. He was becoming family already. He had to be part of my dinner.

"So what's your second question?"

"Which one to make?" He laughed.

"You mean which one for *us* to decide to make?" I asked jokingly, making sure he knew who was in charge.

"Exactly. Let me do some checking into my recipes and we'll pick one together." He looked deep in thought as he turned to leave the kitchen. "Thanks, Cass. This'll be fun."

***

I was going to have my work cut out for me with this cooking thing. I think I planned too many things because I was getting all of the ingredients mixed up in my head. Josh and I settled on a spicy bologna sauce for the spaghetti and Nana made her strudel with Cortland and Macintosh and Granny Smith apples... Dad's fries worked better with red bliss

153

potatoes and the scones used poppy seeds in them... I decided I would not be a chef when I grew up. How did those restaurant cooks keep everyone's dinner straight on a busy night? I would go nuts.

Mom and Ben helped me peel the apples for the strudel and Mom showed me how to blend the dough and crumbs "at gradual speed" with the mixer. Everything was so picky about this recipe, but Ben was psyched that we got to put in raisins, and lots of them.

I waited until Wednesday to call Dad back about the fries and was afraid he'd cancel. But he didn't. We decided to meet at his apartment and make the fries at his place after doing the grocery shopping for the potatoes. We'd have to make them and freeze them because Dad couldn't meet the night before my project was due. I thanked him for not canceling.

***

"What do you think?" Dad said, looking unusually domestic in a red and white checked apron. I think he thought everybody wore aprons when they cooked. It was a nice look for him.

I surveyed the batch of peeled and sliced potatoes. They took forever just to get to this point and we hadn't even fried anything yet. "Looks like enough to me. My whole class can try some."

"Okay, the next step is into the pan..." I asked him to pour the batch into the preheated fry pan since I was afraid to get hot sparks in my eyes. Then I took over and stirred. After all, it was my project.

After a few minutes, Dad laughed, saying "Are we far back enough?" He pointed to my awkward stance almost two feet away from the counter. Flipping the potatoes was near to impossible if you couldn't reach the pan. Without saying anything, Dad slipped out of the kitchen and returned with a pair of old sunglasses.

"Try these," he said, pointing to the pan and back to my face.

I smiled and put them on. Sometimes Dads were smarter than you thought. He obviously understood the situation but didn't make me feel chicken for being afraid of the sparks. Once I put them on, I wasn't afraid to get close to the pan anymore. So what if it was a little dark wearing shades in the house? I was a cool cook and this was a cool project.

The night ended all too early and before long it was time for Dad to drive me home. The only sadness to a perfectly fun evening came when Dad locked up his apartment behind us and we headed out into the windy night. There it was again. The sad, reminder feeling that Dad lived away and my home wasn't his anymore.

Chapter Seventeen
Teamwork

"Ben!" I snapped. "If you're going to stir then you have to get everything all mixed in together." I peered into the bowl of peach-colored scone dough and saw the glob of poppy seeds all piled in the center. "See?" Grabbing the spoon, I scraped and pulled all of the plain dough out from the sides of the mixing bowl.

"Cassie, you don't have to yell at him," Mom said. "He's just trying to help. Remember, this is your project—not his."

"Yeah, I know. Sorry. I just want this to come out really good."

Josh crossed over from the counter where he was laying out the ingredients for the spaghetti sauce and inspected Ben's bowl of dough. "It's going to be awesome, don't you worry," he patted my shoulder.

He leaned in to Ben and whispered, "Pretend they're raisins and you want to make sure everybody gets some in their cookies."

Ben smiled at this. "Okay," he nodded. I should have thought of this. He could relate to raisins.

A couple of times I thought about Dad. He wasn't here now, but at least he got to help. He made my project important enough. For the first time in a long while, I felt truly grateful.

Josh left the kitchen to head for the bathroom. I wanted to use this time before Josh got back.

"Mom, do you ever miss Dad?" I wondered if this was the right time to ask.

She nodded. "Sometimes. I miss the early days. But he's changed, honey. I've changed. Sometimes people get older and things change so much that it's better to go separate ways."

"How do you know if that's going to happen when you marry somebody?"

"You can never know for sure. There are no guarantees. But, you just do the best you can to be a good person and to choose your husband carefully, and a little prayer always helps." Mom smiled.

She was always saying something about God here and there. I think her faith improved over the years because she talks about it much more now than I ever remembered. I guess that's a good thing.

Josh came back and gave Mom a hug as he walked by to rinse off his sauce spoons in the sink. He must have whispered something because Mom whispered back "I love you too," just loud enough for us to hear.

The kitchen smelled good with all of the food but once the scones were baking it was strange with the smells of orange poppy seed scones mixing with spicy bologna sauce on the stove. Almost done now, I could just about relax. Once everything was done cooking, I just had to put it in containers and bring in the crock pots for the pasta and sauce and microwave pans for the scones and fries. We probably should have had a real vegetable thrown in somewhere but I didn't feel like making Mom's recipe for red cabbage with raisins. I never knew a kid who would eat cabbage—with or without raisins.

***

I talked to Marcy on the phone that night.

"You're done, already?" Marcy sounded surprised. I tipped the receiver to my shoulder and held it with my chin as I colored in the rest of my place tags. I had decided to make little tags about each food to put on the buffet table. Each one labeled the food and said something about where the food came from and which family member gave me the recipe. Plus, Mom had photocopied the recipe cards at her work and I just had to cut them up (since there were three on a page) and sort them into piles. All of this was easy to do and still talk to Marcy on the phone.

"Yeah, almost finished, and just in the nick of time. It's almost bedtime."

160

"But it's only a quarter past nine! I'm going to be up all night."

"And why is that, let me ask again?"

"I don't know—why?"

"We've been over this. My best buddy is a last-minute-Annie."

"It's last-minute Marcy to you," she mockingly snapped. "And besides, it's not that I waited on purpose. I just couldn't think of anything good to do. You just got your creative juices going early."

"Well your juice had better start pouring or you'll be bummed in class tomorrow."

She laughed. "I know, my butt's already in gear and this'll be good, trust me. See you tomorrow."

"Bye. And good luck, really."

"Thanks. I may just need it."

Chapter Eighteen
Show Time!

Class was crazy with people lugging in projects and setting
things up on the window ledges and in the kitchen and even
storing things in the closet at the back of Mrs. Frazier's
classroom. Louie Carroll seemed to be the only one who was
so laid back that even the teacher noticed. He wasn't setting
up a thing. He didn't carry anything in. I was convinced he
had just blown it off and decided to flunk instead. What a jerk.
He could have done anything but didn't even bother to try.
Mrs. Frazier would definitely have something to say.

163

Marcy went first. She brought up a big posterboard that had photos taped all over it and each relative was labeled with an astrological sign. She stood at the front of the room and cleared her throat. "Umm hmm. This is a snapshot of my heritage. There's a mixture of backgrounds and I've labeled them here." She pointed to the first picture. Mrs. Frazier leaned forward to see.

"This is my Gramma Pinopoulos," she fingered a photo of a little gray-haired lady with dark eyes. "She's a Taurus. She's stubborn and determined and has to be right ALL of the time."

The class laughed. Mrs. Frazier looked confused but she didn't say anything.

"And this is my Dad's Dad, Grampie MacTavish. He's a Virgo. That makes him quiet and a little shy but he's a great listener especially when you get him alone."

"Marcy, this is wonderful that you've put together a collage of your family members, but what does their heritage have to do with their astrological signs?"

Marcy looked surprised. "Oh, I'm getting to that, Mrs. Frazier, don't you worry."

But I was worried. So far, my buddy hadn't come up with any meaningful heritage research and I thought she had maybe lost her mind being up so late last night. I didn't want her to lose out. She really was smart—it's just she was never really into planning—anything—too far in advance.

She finished her speech about her family members and rested the poster against the blackboard on the chalk tray. The class applauded since we all thought she was finished, but she held up her hands and said "Wait, wait! I'm not done. There's more..."

Mrs. Frazier looked relieved. Everybody liked Marcy and nobody wanted her to fail.

She pulled some papers out of a plastic bag she kept under her desk and started passing them out at the front of each row of desks. "Everybody, please take one and pass it back."

"What is this?" the teacher asked as she accepted a sheet from Marcy.

"This is the heritage part of my project. I told you it was all related—no pun intended." She laughed at her own joke. "This," she continued, is a chart I made up of my family's ancestry and which countries they came from."

This seemed pretty basic enough, but I doubted if it was enough "depth" to satisfy Mrs. Frazier's quest for creative thinking.

"But I didn't stop there, so don't worry."

She smiled at the teacher. What a ham!

"I did some research on racial stereotypes and listed a few in each person's box—like the Irish being known for tempers or Italians labeled as not smart, and so on." Then, I made a new list next to each person's stereotype and wrote in what that person's real traits were for each relative I knew and added some from astrology. Like, I don't remember much about my great-grandmother but Mom told me what she was like and I looked up her birthday and added some of the personality traits of Pisces."

The class looked stunned. Marcy was usually pretty creative and astrology was definitely a stretch, but you had to give her credit—it was original!

"Marcy, I must say I am impressed. Now there are many who think astrology is not exactly scientific but you've done some research and come up with a very creative project. Thank you."

Now even though the teacher was not one to announce grades, I was sure Marcy did really well and could be proud. I thought she did great—and even more so for the last minute. She was such a cool friend.

I went next—not exactly voluntarily though. Marcy pulled my hand up as she returned to her seat and the teacher thought I was answering her call for volunteers.

I said mine would take a few minutes of preparation and could I have someone to help me get things set up. Marcy volunteered and helped me heat everything up in the microwave and set up hot plates on the little card table that Brad had set up first thing in class for anybody who would need it.

Marcy passed out the recipe handouts and I set up the little ID cards next to each food.

"What is this?" Mrs. Frazier gazed at all of the food. She was definitely impressed.

"It's called a Round-the-World Dinner and it tells a story about my family."

"Wow!" somebody from class yelled and I wasn't sure if it was Louie or not but if it was it was probably because he was hungry and not just proud of my idea.

"I come from a family with mostly English and German background, and my Mom's fiancé has some Italian so I added him too."

I checked the class for a reaction. Guess nobody thought divorce and remarriage was anything big. Inside, I let out a big sigh.

Holding up the plate of scones, I said "these are English orange poppy seed scones and they're eaten sometimes for breakfast like we eat muffins in America. Or sometimes people eat them at tea time which can be anytime between 2:00 and 4:00 in the afternoon."

"And this is my Mom's apple strudel, which came from her Mom, my Nana Ochs. She's German, and this is our favorite dessert we have on holidays and sometimes at Sunday dinners a few times during the year."

The kids were being really polite and I felt my voice relax as my worries subsided. I was always afraid of being made fun of –or laughed at.

"These are English fries, they're chunks of potato like home fries but the English call them chips. And this is Josh's—he's my Mom's fiancé—special spicy pasta sauce. He's like a chef and he's Italian and he always makes us guess what's in the sauce." I took a deep breath. This was the part I was afraid would sound goofy but I decided to chance it. "So, if you want, we can have a little contest and see who can guess the most ingredients on this one. I have little slips of paper you can use and..."

Mrs. Frazier piped up "and maybe the winner gets extra credit—or some other prize."

"Extra credit!" Louie cheered and rifled through my recipe cards Marcy had passed out to the class before my presentation.

Brad leaned over and said loudly, "The sauce one ain't in there, Louie. For Heaven's sake, she's not dumb."

The class laughed. I felt my face redden. "Thank you Brad. And no, I left the sauce recipe out."

After they tried the sauce, everyone filled out the slips and turned them in after my speech. We decided to read them later and let everyone finish eating while other people took turns to show their projects.

Louie volunteered—no big surprise—to go next. He walked to the front of the room, swinging his arms.

"And what have we here, Mr. Carroll?"

"Mrs. Frazier, ladies and gentlemen, we have the ultimate in a heritage project. Better than anything I could have made or wrote about or even cooked—no offense, Cassie."

"Which is?" the teacher pressed, cutting short his dramatic moment just a bit.

"Me. Life. A real live, breathing, talking human being."

"Too bad it's not thinking..." somebody snickered from the back.

"Close your mouth, Robertson. It's rude to interrupt," he said primly.

He pointed to the top of his head and announced, "this is my super-curly fantastic Hispanic hair."

The class giggled.

"And this," he gestured to his arm, "is my Italian tan."

"And these, are my Irish eyes." He winked his green eyes back at us.

He smiled, showing all of his teeth. "And I could be wrong, but I have really straight, white teeth, which could be French maybe, since I have some French on my grandmother's side."

"I see," said Mrs. Frazier, nodding. "And do you have any props to go with your human project?"

Louie shook his head, and then seemed to think better of it and crossed over to the black board. "I could draw you my life-size project," he said, standing with his back against the board and trying to trace around his head with a big piece of chalk.

In thirty seconds, he had scrawled a child-like drawing of his eyes, nose, and mouth and labeled each item with a nationality—"Spanish", "French," "Italian", etc.

We waited for Mrs. Frazier to chew him out. Flunk him. Make him take his seat and then lecture him for copping out. But she didn't.

"Well, Mr. Carroll, I must say I am impressed with your ingenuity on this one. While you didn't spend the time that some of the other students have, I will take your creativity into consideration."

That was it! Wow! She really was forward-thinking for a teacher. I think I would have busted him for taking the easy

171

way out. But then again...I guess it took some creativity to think that up—and even more guts to show up with a whopper like that in front of the whole class: the human project.

Chapter Nineteen
Feeling Lucky

At the end of class, I was glad nobody else did food. Ming

Wu's project didn't really count as food—since she only talked

about her Dad's Chinese restaurant, and the little take-out

boxes she brought in had only fortune cookies in them. Of

course, that's the best part of Chinese food, and I'm even

gonna save my fortune. It said "Your horizons are broad and

your dreams within reach."

I waited on the bench outside school for Mom to pick me

up since I couldn't carry all of the crock pots and project stuff

173

on the bus. I guessed there must be traffic since she was late, and most of the other kids had gone home. The assistant principal was just now pulling away in his gray Honda, and the only ones left outside were me, an older kid I didn't know, and—Brad! I wasn't sure how long he was standing by the bike rack. I wondered if he saw me.

Frantically, I sought an excuse to talk to him—but gave it up. I was in a good mood—my project went awesome today—and so what if I just went over to chat? He was a friend, sort of.

"Hi, Brad. You did a good job today."

"Thanks."

"You waiting for your Mom to come get you?"

I eyed his boxes of flats and planters from his Mom's florist shop. He did a cool presentation on his Mom's family history of greenhouses—and traced it all the way back to the potato farmers in Ireland.

"Step-Mom, actually."

"Oh? I must have missed that in your talk."

"No, I don't usually call her my step-Mom 'cause she's really everything a Mom is—she's there for my brother Brent and me, and works and cooks and, you know, takes care of us."

"Sure."

"I just mentioned it because of what you said today—about your parents' divorce."

I still hated that word. "Your parents split up too?"

He nodded. "You could say that," he said. "It's more complicated than that, though—maybe not worth the trouble to tell."

"Try me."

Looking a little surprised at my openness, he straightened up, and said "Okay." He took a deep breath, which made him look a lot older, more serious.

"My Mom died in a car accident when I was four," he said soberly.

"Oh, I'm so sorry," I said, embarrassed now that I had pushed him to talk.

"I know. It was really sad and I missed her a lot but I don't remember as much about her anymore—except for the way she laughed—she had the best laugh in the world." He paused and

175

added, "So my Dad took me and Brent, who was just a baby when Mom died."

"And he got remarried?"

"Yeah—a few years later, to Kate, the lady who owns the florist shop."

"Then what happened?"

"Well, he had a lot of trouble at work, and he started drinking again, and one day he just left. We went to school and he was gone by the time we got home."

"Oh, my God."

"It's okay. I was real mad for a long time—this was three years ago—and then I was afraid Kate would leave us, too."

"Did you ever tell her?"

"Yeah—one time after another nightmare. She said she wasn't the type to quit anything she'd started and that me and Brent were the best things that ever happened to her."

"She sounds wonderful."

"She is—and you know what? I couldn't have imagined a nicer Mom. She really loves us."

"So that's why you did your project on her background— she's a real Mom to you now."

He looked away, scanning the parking lot. "She's my only Mom, really. I mean, here. But I bet my real Mom would really like her."

"Where's your Dad now?" I asked tentatively, surprised he was confiding in me.

"Don't know. I hope someday he'll come back but I'm not expecting it. Kate's not mad at him but she cries sometimes and tells us that Dad really tried, but he just couldn't get over Mom dying on us and him being left alone with two kids."

"Do you hate him sometimes?"

"I did at first, but not anymore. I think it must have been really hard on him when Mom died. I just think I was lucky he stayed long enough to find us a new Mom."

"Wow..."

"What?"

"It's just—that's so amazing. You've been through so much and you don't even hold a grudge."

"It's because I'm lucky. One day, I stopped and thought about it—that when people have been in my life, they've loved me and made it better."

"But they left…" I protested, suddenly beginning to feel lucky too, since my parents were still around.

"But I wasn't *alone*," he insisted. "I was never left totally alone and it made me really trust that everything would be all right."

"Wow. Guess I'm lucky too. It's taken a long time for me to stop feeling cheated because it's so weird seeing my Mom and Dad in two different places and not having them there all the time. But at least I have them—they're still my Mom and Dad—no matter what." I was glad he reminded me about how lucky I really am. "Thanks, Brad. Hey, you sound really together for 13."

He smiled. "Well that's a little secret too. Before we moved here, I had to stay back since I missed so much school after Dad left. You know, going to counselors and sorting things out."

I nodded, wondering how he made it through all of this. "I'm 14."

"Oh. Well, you still sound really mature for 14."

"Thanks."

***

I thought about my new friend after Brad's step-Mom came to pick him up. He's been through way more than I could ever imagine—and he still felt "lucky". I found myself focusing on the word over and over in my head—*lucky...lucky...lucky.*

Suddenly, I felt silly about all of the things I'd been thinking lately. Sure, it wasn't perfect, but at least my Mom and Dad loved me. The soft whirr of Dad's engine broke my thoughts as it pulled in the long driveway to the school and circled around in front of the building. It was Dad! What was he doing here?

I ran over to the car. "Dad? Hi!"

"Hi, honey. I came to get you since your Mom called and she's stuck at an appointment. How did your project go?"

He remembered! "It was great, Dad" I said, opening the passenger door and sliding into the seat beside him. "We made everything and everybody loved the fries."

"They did? Oh, I'm so glad, honey. Sorry we had to freeze them a few days early, but we got it done, didn't we?" He nudged me in the arm.

"We sure did," I smiled, secretly feeling lucky. "Thanks."

Chapter Twenty
My Family Tree

"Ouch!" I hollered, a little louder than necessary, to my

empty room. The hot glue from the gun seemed to seal in the

burn on my thumb, and I tried to slurp the heat out by sucking

on it. My tree was almost finished—I had beat around the

bush long enough—and I was finally ready to get down to work

and turn it in to Mrs. Frazier. Most of my tags were glued

lightly on each branch, so that they dangled, and the slightest

breeze made them look like little paper leaves.

All of the aunts, uncles, grandparents, and cousins were in place. Mom was glued, Ben was tagged and I was sticking him on right now, and all that was left were Dad and Josh. Dad had been moved around practically every day since I'd started this silly tree, and I was tired of agonizing over the whole thing. I thought about Mom's sparkling new ring from Josh. The wedding would be here in a few months—after school got out, a little after my thirteenth birthday.

Since the engagement was official, I placed Josh gently beside Mom on the parents' branch—he looked pretty good there. For Mom and Josh and Ben, I decided to put pictures with their tags to make the tree more personal, more lively.

I knelt lower into the carpet to inspect the tree. Most of the limbs were full with paper "leaves", and the tree was looking quite nice, I had to admit. My knees were starting to hurt from squatting and kneeling so long over the tree, but it wouldn't be long now. I leaned to peek under the bed, and retrieved my weekend-long "surprise" from its box in the corner. The idea had taken weeks to think up, and hours to finish. I hadn't even told Marcy—or Mom or Dad or Josh—for that matter. But it didn't matter anymore—I had found a way. Everybody would be on my tree, since that was the whole point of Family Month.

Eyeing the little popsicle-stick structure I had stained with brown shoe polish, I positioned Dad's name-tag on the front door and glued the tiny building to the main "parents" branch. Feeling proud of my creative thinking, I shifted the tree to inspect the base and thought of one last addition. I decided to collect one last nature specimen from outside before abandoning the project for bed. It was late and I was tired, but this was so exciting. Just weeks ago, the tree was a nightmare and I got stomachaches thinking about it. Everything had been such a mess, but now it would be okay. All of it would turn out all right.

***

Class was buzzing with kids bringing in the last of their Family Month projects—the infamous family tree—and my tree would be first, since we drew numbers by lottery and I was the lucky one to start off the tree presentations. I wasn't as nervous anymore, mostly because the other day went so well with my Round-the-World dinner.

"Hey—Cass!"

"What?" It was Louie, yelling at me from two rows over.

"Mrs. F, she gave me extra credit for guessing your sauce!"

"She did? Great!"

"Yeah—saved me! Thanks."

"Sure." Leave it to Louie to always land on his feet. Wait 'til Josh hears his spaghetti sauce saved Louie Carroll from flunking English.

Mrs. Frazier cleared her throat and called the class to attention. "Are you ready, Cassidy?"

"Yes," I said confidently, and walked to the front of the room. Holding up my creation, I smiled and announced "This is my family tree."

"Would you like to walk us through it?" she asked me.

"Sure. I wanted the tree to look as natural as possible— because families are natural—so that's why I decided to make the tree out of a real tree, with branches and bark, and wood." I looked over at Marcy, who was smiling back at me with encouragement.

"I like it. Very earthy," said Mrs. Frazier.

"Thank you. And these tags are just paper but they're glued on to look like leaves so they dangle…"

"And you have names on them?"

"Yes. These are my great grandparents at the top, and then my Grandma and Grandpa, and on the opposite side are Nana and Poppa…" I pointed down to the lower levels of the tree. "And over here are my cousins Tia and Jody and Chris—and my Aunt Jillian and Uncle Ted…"

I pointed to the biggest, thickest branch on the tree. "And this is my main branch—Mom's here, see—she's connected down to me and my brother Ben…and next to her is her fiancé, Josh… They're getting married this May…"

Catching Marcy's gaze again, I noticed she was still smiling at me. She was such a supportive friend.

"And what have we here?" Mrs. Frazier leaned over to inspect the little building seated on the branch next to Mom and Josh.

"This," I explained slowly, "is a tree-house." A few kids laughed. I guess my idea was a little different… "For my Dad." The kids stopped laughing. "He's still my Dad but he doesn't live at home anymore."

Mrs. Frazier smiled, "so you've built him a wonderful place in your family tree. What creative thinking here!"

I could tell she was proud. I was even proud.

"And what's this at the base?" She fingered some clumps of green I had glued to the bottom of the tree. "A lawn?"

"No. It's clover. For luck. A friend reminded me the other day of how lucky I was to have such a wonderful family." I glanced in Brad's direction. He was smiling at me.

"Now, that's a family tree," said Mrs. Frazier.

I nodded. It sure was.

About the Author

Sandra Lee Churchill is a writer, poet, and communications specialist who authors articles on parenting, community news, and topics of general interest. Several of her poems have been published in St. Anthony Messenger magazine, and hundreds of her articles have appeared in regional newspapers as well as business and professional publications. She makes her home in Massachusetts with her husband and three children.